DISCARD

The Smell of Old Lady Perfume

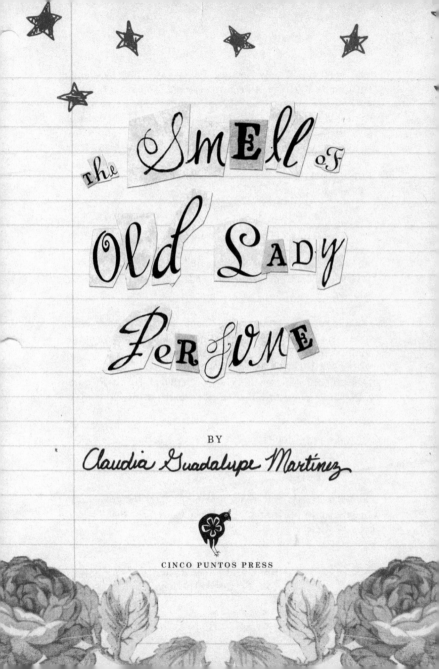

THE SMELL OF OLD LADY PERFUME

BY

Claudia Guadalupe Martinez

CINCO PUNTOS PRESS

FIRST EDITION
10 9 8 7 6 5 4 3

Library of Congress Cataloging-in-Publication Data

Martínez, Claudia Guadalupe, 1978-
  The smell of old lady perfume / by Claudia Guadalupe Martínez.
— 1st ed.
        p. cm.
  Summary: When sixth grader Chela Gonzalez's father has a stroke and her grandmother moves in to help take care of the family, her world is turned upside down.
  ISBN 978-1-933693-88-0 (alk. paper)
  [1. Family life–Fiction. 2. Schools–Fiction. 3. Death–Fiction. 4. Hispanic Americans–Fiction. 5. Grandmothers–Fiction.] I. Title.

PZ7.M36714Sm 2008
[Fic]--dc22

                                        2007038296

Thanks to Jessica Powers for helping us enter the great world of young adult books and for her good eye on *The Smell of Old Lady Perfume*.

**Book and cover design
by Sergio A. Gómez**

for my family

Apá was a strong still oak.
We hid under his branches like shadows.
Even when he laughed a thunderous laugh,
those branches shook only ever so slightly.

ALL ABOUT the SIXTH GRADE

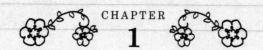

CHAPTER
1

Apá told me to imagine that sixth grade was like standing at the top of the tallest building downtown. It was like being up there in that tall building and looking down. The people on the street looked just like ants. To sixth graders, those ants were fifth graders, fourth graders, third graders, all the way down to pre-kindergarteners. Each grade was farther away than the next, smaller than the last. The best thing was—those ants looked up to sixth graders. Knowing this made me all the more nervous and excited about starting sixth grade.

Sixth grade was a big deal where I lived because it marked our last year of elementary school. Some people may be too old to remember or too young to imagine, but my older brother Angel Jr. remembered. He and my sister Silvia, the twins, had been sixth graders two years before me.

I clung to any sliver of information about their fascinating lives back then. Angel Jr. bragged that being a sixth grader was like being a big brother.

Everyone wanted to be like you, and you bossed them around. Sixth graders sat in the front row of the cafeteria and got dibs on the best foods. According to him, he once took a slice of meatloaf right off a fourth grader's plate because that was the one that made his mouth water.

Sixth graders checked out any book they wanted to in the library too, even the special books the librarian locked in her office—the ones that explained the stuff we'd talked about once the year before during P.E. There were no tables to share in the classroom or trying to avoid a neighbor's elbow in the middle of a test either. Each kid got a desk with a writing table attached and book basket underneath, like the ones in high school. It was the best of everything.

I wanted my sister Silvia to tell me about sixth grade too. I thought that us being sisters meant she would share all the secret things only girls knew, but the only thing we shared was our room, and that was because my parents made her. She and

Angel Jr. just weren't the same. It wasn't always that one twin was good and one was bad, like in the movies. They were more like different parts of the same thing, like a pencil and an eraser. Sometimes they worked together; sometimes they didn't.

There were other ways they were supposed to be alike, but weren't. Angel Jr. was as tall as a man. Silvia was small like me. In the same way that Clark and I had Apá's too-broad smile, baked skin and serious eyes, the twins both had olive skin and black hair like our mom. But while Angel Jr. had a big nose and one million freckles, Silvia had a regular nose and a smooth face.

I promised myself that when I got to be old like Silvia, or older, I wouldn't be like her other than in the way that she dressed. I'd be nicer. I'd talk to everyone, like my dad and Angel Jr. always did. It didn't matter that my dad's English was rough. Apá would have talked to the president of the United States himself just as easily as he talked to the guy asking for change on the corner. I wanted to be like that. I wanted to be able to talk to anyone and give advice about school to younger kids. I especially wanted to give advice to any girls that might ask. I promised myself that when I got into seventh and eighth grade, I'd let younger girls know just what sixth grade was like.

I tried very hard to copy Silvia in other ways, though, the ones I imagined mattered in school. We were allowed to pick out new school outfits at the end of the summer. We each got small allowances, and took turns going shopping during different weeks. When my turn came to pick out my sixth grade wardrobe, I told my parents that I didn't want to go to Penneys. It was the only department store Downtown. I asked Amá to take me to the Korean stores on Stanton Street just like Silvia had done. Everything there was cheap. I chose things that I'd seen Silvia and her friends buying. I got red leather sneakers, one size too big. Those, my mom stuffed with cotton for me to grow into. I got four pairs of jeans and a bunch of different-colored T-shirts for every day of the week. I even got a skirt for special occasions like the first day of school. It was the jean type and long enough to hide the spider-shaped soccer scars on my knees.

I loved soccer. My whole family had played soccer together at the park since I could remember. When we didn't play, we watched. I played at school too. There was a P.E. tournament for every grade every spring. The winning teams got pizza parties and bragging rights. I hadn't been to a pizza party yet, but I knew sixth grade would be different.

When my best friend Nora came over on our last weekend of summer, I pulled out my soccer ball. We kicked it around and talked about what it'd be like to win the soccer tournament. "If we played with just two people on each team, we'd win for sure. You're fast and I'm strong. Wouldn't that be great?" I asked.

"Yeah, but a pizza party wouldn't be that great

with just two of us," she answered, wiping the sweat off her glasses with her T-shirt. "We can do that anytime."

She was probably right, but it would've still been fun. I always had a good time when Nora was around. We'd known each other since the first grade, and had become inseparable right away, like melted cheese on tortilla chips. We laughed and told each other everything.

Most of my expectations about sixth grade had actually come from Nora. She'd learned everything she needed to know about sixth grade at Science Camp, which was summer school for kids who loved that stuff. She had gone there for six weeks during the summer, though none of what she'd learned seemed to have anything to do with science.

Nora had found out that we were going to be in the smart class, the A-class, together. They only spoke English in that class. We'd never been in a class like that before. Even though my parents pressed me to learn more and more English, they still only talked Spanish at home. I sometimes struggled if I tried to speak like those A-class kids. My Spanish popped through like slices of color on a yellow wall that'd been painted white. I'd always ended up in the bilingual classes because of that. It wasn't that there was something wrong with bilingual classes, but A-class kids did seem to think they were smarter. Everyone knew their names, and other kids definitely wanted to be like them.

Being in the A-class meant everyone would know our names too.

"Chela Gonzalez," Nora said as she got ready to go home. "This year is going to be different. We're A-class now. This year, we're going to be painfully popular!"

Talking to Apá

CHAPTER
2

One of the major things Nora had told me was that Camila, the most popular girl in our grade, was moving to a private school. Camila had always been the queen of our grade. With her gone, someone else might actually have a shot at winning the All-School Girl Trophy. According to Angel Jr., only the smartest and most popular girl and boy in school ever won the All-School Trophies.

My thoughts raced around and around that trophy. I decided I wanted to win it real bad. Every time I thought about it, I felt short of breath like when we ran on the school soccer field. I imagined what it would be like to walk up to the cafeteria stage when the principal called out my name as the All-School Girl at the awards assembly. I'd have on a new blouse and my hair would bounce when I turned my head to thank him. I'd be the next Camila, the smart and pretty one everyone looked up to. Even while I celebrated the rumor of Camila's endless summer, the one she'd never return from, I still wanted to be like her.

My excitement grew and grew so much I thought I might pass out from all the running in my head. It was already nighttime and too late to call Nora. But talking to my dad usually helped me see things better.

So the night before sixth grade started, I walked into the living room and found Apá sitting on the floor. He was reading the Spanish-language newspaper and drinking his favorite drink, a tall glass of milk with lots of ice in it. I quick kissed him on the brown of his left cheek. He turned his head toward me—wearing the hat he sometimes wore even indoors to cover his baldness. My thoughts spilled out like marbles rolling everywhere. I spoke so fast that I stumbled on my words and had to repeat myself. I told Apá what Angel Jr. had said about the All-School Trophy. I told him how much I wanted to win. I knew that with Camila gone, I could do it.

Apá didn't say anything at first. He sat there thinking for awhile, the way he always did. He breathed deeply and stared into space as if he could see something important. He fiddled with his pack of cigarettes and tucked one behind his ear like a pen. Then he turned back to me. "Chela, be proud of who you are. You're going to win that trophy because you'll work hard to be the smartest. It doesn't matter who your competition is."

"¡*Sí*, Apá! But now it's definitely going to be easier," I insisted.

"You know," Apá said, "when I was your age my father wouldn't let me go to school because we couldn't pay to go into the city to study. He was a poor farmer and too proud to let me take a scholarship. Most people where we came from only made it to the sixth grade. But even when I couldn't go to school anymore, I read everything I could get my hands on." He snapped the pages of his newspaper to make his point. "I never stopped learning."

I understood what Apá was saying. I needed to push myself no matter what, even if there was no school or no Camila. The only way to win the All-School Trophy was to work hard.

Later that night, we watched an old cowboy movie on Canal Cinco, the Spanish channel. Apá asked me if I wanted to be a cowgirl. I said the first thing that popped into my head. I told him maybe I wanted to be a mom and giggled. He didn't laugh. He told me it was a hard a job. Being a parent was like being a teacher but the after-school bell never rang. Of course, my dad made it look easy. But he also always told the truth. It made me want to be something like a lawyer or a doctor instead.

"Go to bed, mija," Apá said after a while. "I'll wake you up early at six, right after I get up." I kissed him goodnight. When I walked through the living room, Amá was laying out our first-day-of-school outfits on the red couch. There were slacks and a blouse for my sister, baggy pants and T-shirts for my older brother and little brother, and a skirt and a tee for me. My dad's work clothes were there too. I kissed Amá goodnight.

I walked up the stairs into my room and pulled on my pajamas. I climbed into the top bunk bed. I fell asleep and dreamt about the first day of my last year in elementary school. I dreamt that when Nora and I got to school everybody loved us and everything was perfect. Our hair and clothes were perfect. Our team won the big soccer tournament. We got straight A's. Everyone either knew who we were or wanted to know us. We were the new queens.

It was all perfect, except it didn't actually happen like that.

the DARKNESS

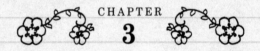

CHAPTER
3

I opened my eyes to a sun already stamped on the sky. I knew instantly that more than the sun was up. There was no wake-up call as promised. It made me angry. Apá had forgotten, and we were going to be late for our first day of school.

I nudged Silvia awake. I unhinged my jaw to complain. Then it hit me: this had never happened. My dad ALWAYS woke us up, ever since I could remember. He woke us up even when there wasn't any school.

"Where's dad?" I asked Silvia.

"I don't know," she yawned, "maybe he overslept. He just finished that big job."

My dad renovated houses—he made big fancy rooms with clean wood floors and shiny marble tile in neighborhoods with green lawns and no chain link fences. His days had been longer and harder than usual.

I climbed out of bed, thinking that I would check on him before getting ready for school. Silvia must've thought of the same thing because she pushed me aside and hurried out of the room in front of me. It wasn't a trick to try and hog the bathroom. She headed straight down the stairs.

When she reached the bottom of the stairs, Silvia brought both her hands over her mouth. "What happened?" she squeaked.

Apá lay frozen on the large furry brown rug in front of his bed, with Amá and Angel Jr. leaning over him. My mom held Apá's hand and tried hard to look calm, but her eyebrows stretched too far up on her forehead for that to be true. Angel Jr.'s face scrunched up too, and his freckles looked like they were about to jump ship.

Angel Jr. spoke fast, fattening up the minutes with words. "I heard this thump. I jumped out of bed. 'Who's there,' I yelled. Then I saw Apá slumped over in the hallway. Amá rushed out of her room too. We pulled him in here and tried to lift him onto the bed, but he was too heavy."

"But what happened?" Silvia repeated.

"I don't know," Angel Jr. said.

Maybe he had fallen and hit his head. If he had, he wasn't saying so. His eyes were open, but he wasn't getting up.

Apá's chin was smooth, so I knew he'd been up before the sun. He always shaved in the upstairs bathroom, the one with the full-sized mirror. He'd probably come down the stairs carefully and quietly when he was done, one step at a time, to get the clothes Amá'd laid out for him on the couch. It couldn't have been much different than other days, except for maybe he'd tripped or gotten dizzy. Only he hadn't called for help.

"Apá," I urged. "Please get up and go to work. Get dressed. Put on your work jeans, and take us to school. I'll help you lace up your boots. Please."

"I can't move," Apá slurred when he finally opened his mouth. "I don't feel myself inside myself."

"Mari?" he called out. My mom squeezed his hand hard, not letting go. "Mari, I want to talk to the kids."

We gathered around him like what my grandma called a circle of penitents. My mom pushed gently at my arm, but I didn't know what else to say. I'd been sideswiped by a dark feeling that only sank me deeper when I remembered I'd been angry with him when I woke up. Apá whispered to Angel Jr. to take care of us. He kissed each of us. "You go to school now and work hard," he said. I bit the inside of my cheek until the taste of copper told me there was blood. I didn't let out another peep. I held very still because I didn't want to do the wrong thing. I didn't want him to know I was scared that he was saying goodbye when no one was going anywhere, not even school.

"I was born near the waters of the Rio Florido," he said. The river, which had since turned into more of a dry creek, was named after the town where he and Amá grew up. "I'm going to close my eyes and wake up in those waters."

There was panic on Amá's face when he said those things. It was like that time when she had a headache that wouldn't go away no matter how many Tylenol she took. She went to the doctors who told her she had a brain tumor. She thought she was going to die. She told Apá that she couldn't believe Diosito would let her leave us without a mother. She was right. Pretty soon her belly started to outgrow her shirt. She didn't have a tumor—God was just sending us my little brother.

The look on Amá's face was that same look. It was a look that asked God how He could leave us without a father. But then her face changed. It was like someone had thrown a bucket of ice cold water on her, and she finally woke up.

"You're not going anywhere. Don't close your eyes. We're right here with you. You're going to be fine. You're going to be fine!" she told Apá. She held his head and rocked fast and light like a cicada's wing. She ground her teeth, and I could tell she was trying hard not to cry, trying to hold herself. Only her body fluttered. She hummed that sound she did when we were sick or hurting. She refused to let him sink into the darkness.

"We're taking you to get help," Amá said.

Apá tried to smile, but only one corner of his mouth cooperated.

Amá continued to hold Apá and rock.

Angel Jr. went into the living room and dialed 911.

Silvia sat on the bed and whispered to Clark who was just waking up.

I didn't listen to anything else. It was like walking far into a tunnel or a thought. I lay down on the floor, at the end of the rug, and held my wet face against the bottom of Apá's bare feet. I was sure that he could feel me hugging him, even if his body couldn't feel anything else. I held very still and heard only the sirens of the ambulance coming to get Apá.

Sick days

CHAPTER
4

Amá said she wanted us at home so the house wouldn't be empty and sad to return to. I was sure the house would be sad whether we went to school or stayed home. The truth was she didn't want to have to pull us out of class if things got worse, so she called us in sick.

"I'm going with you," Angel Jr. said. But the ambulance driver wouldn't let him get in. We couldn't go to the hospital. No kids under the age of fifteen were allowed to visit. It had something to do with younger kids always getting sick. We shared colds, flus and other germs at school. They didn't want us sharing these with people who were already sick. Since we hadn't been to school, I wasn't sure this had anything to do with us. We hadn't even had the chance to meet any dangerous germs.

"What do we do then?" Silvia asked.

"Wait," Amá said. She told us to stay off the phone in case she called and make like summer had never ended. But how could we do that with Apá sick?

All summer long we'd waited outside for Apá to come home from work because his return was the best part of the day.

Once after he came home, when a few warm drops from a few black clouds fell, we didn't run inside. We held hands in a circle instead and skipped around, singing: *Que llueva, que llueva, la Virgen de la cueva, los pajarillos cantan, la luna se levanta.* "Let it rain, let it rain, the Virgin in the cave, the birds do sing, the moon rising." Apá called it a rain dance for people who also went to Mass and believed in saints. When the water finally came drumming down and our backyard flooded, we followed the puddles. Apá grabbed giant pieces of flat wood from his wood pile and we pretended they were rafts— even after they sank when they hit the water. We giggled until our lips and toes turned blue.

Another time we waited, it was so hot outside that the pavement felt like a frying pan on our bare feet, so we made like it was Día de San Juan. St. John was the one who baptized Jesus Christ. On that fake Día de San Juan, Apá got out of his truck, untangled the hose, turned it on, put his thumb over the hose's opening, and baptized us all over with cold water. Then he sprayed water up into the air and made a rainbow.

We ran under Apá's rainbow until the backyard was like a soup bowl of mud. When I saw Angel Jr.'s hands dig into the soggy brown, I jumped out of the way. I ran behind Apá, hoping for protection. Sblat! There wasn't any protection and a ball of mud hit me right in the face. Apá didn't let it go any farther because I was complaining, and it made Amá furious when we dirtied up clothes anyway.

Most days, Apá let us drink the leftover coffee he brought home in his thermos. He sat with us out on the back porch on his old log bench and watched as we mixed in three parts milk and as much sugar as could melt in room temperature coffee. We added ice. *Café con leche me quiero casar*...it started a song about a girl who wanted a husband. All we wanted was the coffee. We shook, shook, shook it, while we danced around the yard. We poured it into tiny porcelain cups that Silvia carefully washed, dried and put away in the dining room cabinet. We drank up. My dad's leftovers made a sweet delicious coffee-flavored milk that went down smooth. Silvia allowed herself to be a kid, but made herself feel better by giving it a fancy name like "afternoon tea." It was an idea she got from a ladies magazine.

But when the ambulance came and took my dad away and we sat there waiting for him to come home, there was no dancing for the rain, no mud, and no tea party. Angel Jr. played video games. Clark made a cardboard welcome-home poster with the art set Silvia got for Christmas. Silvia read a book. I watched television.

By the afternoon, I really started to wish we'd gone to school or at least to the hospital. Angel Jr. disappeared and later told us that he'd tried to sneak in to see Apá. He was tall enough to pass for a grown-up, but the front desk clerk had told him no just like the ambulance driver had.

We lounged around the house all day as we pleased, and with each passing hour, the ceiling dropped closer and closer. Eventually it was a house with a ceiling only two feet high so that even if we were free to do anything, there was no room or desire to move.

Finally I got off the couch and stood over Silvia. I looked over her shoulder until she turned around. She was annoyed, but I asked anyway. "Do you think Apá is coming back?"

"Don't even think that he's not!" she snapped and threw the book at me as she stomped away.

When Amá came home she told us they were keeping Apá at the hospital, and she didn't know when he'd be back. She told us he had stopped talking but was thinking of us every minute he was there. Then she started calling people and letting them know about Apá.

The hours became days, and my grandma, on

my mom's side, showed up and set up camp at our house. Abuelita lived a nine-hour bus ride away in El Florido and was the only grandma we knew. A handful of smiling pictures in our photo album hinted that we liked her once. She was an older version of my mom, one built like a washing machine, one more strict and religious than a nun, one who sometimes seemed to love church even more than she loved God. She wasn't all bad though—she told my mom that she should let us go back to school. But Amá had already made up her mind that we wouldn't return to school until my dad came home.

So the days passed and nothing much changed, except that the air became thick with the smell of old lady perfume, of dying flowers and alcohol. It was the same smell from when my mom was sick with my little brother. It was the smell of bad things.

LA FE

Amá let Silvia and me tag along with her to La Fe. La Fe was our neighborhood clinic. We went there when we weren't feeling good or when we needed our teeth cleaned or for a checkup or shots.

My mom wanted to talk to Dr. Gutierrez, our family's regular doctor. He spoke Spanish, and she was sure he'd be able to help her better than the hospital doctors who seemed to be talking to her down their noses like she'd just crossed the river.

La Fe wasn't far enough from our house to get a ride. It was far enough to make me wish it were though. We couldn't drive there either because Amá had never learned how to. She'd only ever seen two cars growing up, and those two cars had crashed one day in front of the plaza and in front of almost all the four hundred people who lived in El Florido. It'd left a big impression. She walked as much as possible, except for taking the bus once in a while or letting my dad drive her places.

Amá was the fastest-walking grown-up in the world. Her calves were strong and curved. There was no medal or anything, but she acted like she was running a race. She got us everywhere faster than a bus. When we complained, she told us we "weren't born in a car."

It was afternoon when we started walking to La Fe. The school bus with the kids who were too little to walk home by themselves drove up beside us. I'd been on that bus just a couple of few years before. The blur of yellow made me wish I were still riding with the little kids. Being on that bus would've meant Apá was all right.

I ground my heels into the pavement as if it hurt to go anywhere. It was hot outside. My shirt already clung to the underside of my arms and my socks were wet inside my shoes. "Pick up your feet," Amá said to me. She hated when I dragged my feet. I dragged my feet even more.

"Hurry—and stop dragging. Those are your

new shoes," Amá repeated as we got closer and closer to the clinic.

When we got to La Fe, Silvia and I waited outside the door while Amá went into Dr. Gutierrez's office. We eavesdropped through the open door. We overhead him say something went wrong inside Apá. A clot in his head cut the oxygen going to his brain. That's why he couldn't move. It was called a stroke. Dr. Gutierrez had talked to the doctors at the hospital and heard that Apá was holding on.

Amá started to tell the doctor Apá's life story. "Surviving is in his blood," my mom told him. She told him how much Apá had gone through when he was young. "His own mother died of cancer when he was only a baby." Apá never talked about her, but we'd heard the story anyway from my other grandmother who'd known his family growing up.

My dad's mom hadn't wanted to die. She was a smart girl from the capital and knew what cancer was. She knew it wasn't like a cold or a stomachache.

My grandfather would tell her not to cry, and then cry himself. She died maybe dreaming of that young son who she wasn't meant to love.

My grandpa Francisco died several years later from what people believed was a broken heart. Completely orphaned at the age of thirteen, Apá lost everything. Their farm went to the bank. His sister Tina had grown up and left long before. Apá went from neighbor to neighbor helping out in exchange for a place to sleep and eventually saved up enough money to ride the rail lines up the Mexican desert to California. He was flung into a world of Levi jeans, brilliantine, English, and confusion. People whispered that they didn't believe any good could come of a boy alone, set loose in the world. They told him he'd never grow up to be a man. But he did grow up.

He followed my aunt to Los Angeles. They had never been close, but that quickly changed. Aunt Tina's husband worked construction and from him

Apá learned a skill. Apá eventually moved to El Paso and started a family of his own. He worked odd jobs until he started a construction business himself.

My father survived.

My mom told the doctor that my father hadn't stepped into a doctor's office since the days of his boyhood. Maybe it was on account of his parent's death that he didn't trust doctors much. He'd stayed away from them for years.

Even when we were born, he'd kept his distance. "Angel just waited in the waiting room. He sat there and declared that's what waiting rooms were for," Amá told the doctor. She told him instead of visiting clinics, Apá read all about plants and their healing powers. If he coughed, he sipped lime juice and honey. If his stomach turned sour, he ate mint.

He even swallowed a clove of garlic every night, believing it kept him healthy. He'd fallen off a roof on a job without breaking a bone. He'd been okay after being bitten by a black widow that had crawled out of the kitchen sink after spending months getting fat in the pipes. Every time he came out standing, he thanked the garlic.

It didn't mean he was a health nut. He still ate bad food for lunch at work, the kind you buy from the window of a truck and eat in a car. And—he smoked too many cigarettes.

"But he's a good man!"

That's what Amá wanted the doctor to know most of all. "I'm telling you all of this because he's always taken care of us, and now we're going to take care of him. We're going to get him better," she said.

Amá wanted to know what to expect. Dr. Gutierrez told her it was different for every patient. "Those are particulars you have to discuss with the hospital, if he gets better. I'm sorry. We just have to wait and see." But that's what we'd been doing all along. Amá shook his hand and thanked him anyway.

"I just wanted to scream at that guy! My dad is going to get better. He just has to," Silvia whispered to me as we walked back home.

My father held on.

Prayer

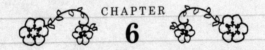

CHAPTER
6

Sunday morning rolled around.

A Sunday could be like a regular day. You could maybe even have fun on a Sunday. But I was feeling sadder than ever because at the end of the day, Sunday meant another week. It meant starting all over again and more of the same.

My dad hadn't gotten any worse, but he also hadn't gotten any better.

Wishing for Apá to get better was like standing at the bottom of a crater and calling out but only our own voices called back. It was pointless. Because we couldn't just wish, we prayed. So, though we didn't go to Mass, we went to the church.

It was a lot for us to even be doing that much. My mom usually had to spoon-force church on us. She nagged and nagged and that mostly made us want to go less, like when she would bug us to do the dishes. She kept telling us until it made us not want to do it even more.

May was the only time we went to service

willingly. Every day in May, every girl under the age of fifteen put on a dress and veil and went to church after school. Amá called it "Mary Service." We walked up the church's center aisle with handfuls of white daisies and carnations.

The flowers were for the Virgencita's altar. I even kind of liked it. I just had to make sure to be far back enough in line to avoid being pinched by Miss Mickey. She was the lady who lit the candles, passed out the flowers, and got friendly with the priest. She was a dried up *cascarita*, a shell of a woman. She wanted us to walk lightly, stand up straight, and hold our flowers as if we were offering a prayer to God. If we didn't, she pinched us with the bite of a vicious tiny ant grabbing enough skin to make a painful point without leaving a bruise.

I wasn't surprised to see Miss Mickey at the back of the church when we walked in to pray for Apá. I sat in one of the front aisles with my brothers and sister. My super-religious grandma had stayed home. She had actually been to Mass already, and someone needed to be there in case Amá called. The phone had been ringing all day—my mom's sisters from Juarez, my aunt Tina from California, the guys from Apá's work. Besides, Abuelita didn't mind that we went to church alone as long as we went. "Just get closer to God," she said.

I crossed myself. I knelt. I searched my mind for words. I couldn't think of what to say. My mind wandered.

Our church wasn't a square church with white walls. It was a fortress built long before Miss Mickey was born, long before Texas was part of the United States. It smelled old—old wood, old incense, and the awful smell of old women.

There was plenty to look at. There were regular church-type things like wall murals, statues of saints and colored glass. If I squinted, I could even see the nuns praying behind the screens on both sides of the altar. The church was part of a convent, and the nuns prayed there several times a day and sang for special services. If I squeezed my eyes shut and concentrated, I could hear them singing. They were songbirds whose language I didn't understand, but I liked the echoes of their voices. Church wasn't so bad when they were around. Still, on most days, sitting in church was a test no matter how many birds sang.

I bent the tip of my left foot to the back of my right knee and switched feet. I watched Silvia with her hands clasped tightly. I knew that I should be praying too, but I wasn't sure how to start.

"I hope you study harder than you pray," Miss Mickey said. She'd come up right behind me. She wrapped her white shawl tight around her thin shoulders.

I unloaded the first thing that popped into my

head. "Miss Mickey, if people are married in the eyes of God forever, how can a widow like you ever hope to get married again?"

I don't know why I talked back to her. Maybe I was angry that she'd reminded me about school.

"God is going to turn your tongue to pork rinds for talking like that!" Miss Mickey chastised. I knew God wouldn't turn my tongue to *chicharrones*. She said that to kids all the time, and everyone still had tongues made of flesh. What I said was rude, and I was sorry anyway.

"I'm sorry, Miss Mickey," I told her. "It's just that my dad is sick, and..."

"Don't say anything else. The best way to get good things to happen is to be a good person. Stop thinking up nonsense and think of good things, Chela," she said. She pushed the glasses with the half-frames and hanging chain up the bridge of her long nose.

I whispered a thank-you to her. I turned back to the front of the church. I crossed myself. I crossed myself one more time. I tried to think about my dad without the scary parts that were half-true and half-imagination. I shut my eyes so tight I saw flashing colors. I saw his face. I slipped in my request—

"Dear God, I want to be a good person. My dad is a good person. He really is. He's always looking out for everybody. Please look out for him. Please help him to get better. Please, Please, PLEASE. Amen."

I repeated it in the way a person might do with a Hail Mary after confession. I wasn't sure how else to go about it.

When we got home, nothing had happened. I wanted so badly for it to be different, but...the smell of my grandmother's perfume reminded me that she was still there and my dad was still sick.

It was sad like Sundays. It didn't matter if you were sick of Sundays. When they came at you, there wasn't much you could do. They just were.

The Seventh Day

CHAPTER
7

The evening of the seventh day, something finally changed. A pair of doctors wearing mint-colored pajamas came out of my dad's room at the hospital and told my mom that the difficult part was over. They were letting Apá out on Tuesday.

My mom came home that night and told us he'd started talking again. He missed us and couldn't wait to be back.

The wait was unbearable, but this time it was without the question mark that had sent all the angry blood rushing to Silvia's face. There was no more, "Do you think Apá is coming back?"

On Tuesday afternoon, Amá rolled my apá into our living room in a blue vinyl wheel chair on loan from the hospital. He wore the warm-ups that he always wore around the house when he wasn't working. The baseball cap that usually covered his bald head sat on his lap. His hair had turned ash-colored. He looked tired. His smile pulled downward, but there was something in his eyes. To me he still looked like he could do anything and everything.

I looked at my brothers and then at Amá. When no one opened their mouth, I ran to Apá's side. I hugged him tight, tight, tight, to give him everything I'd held onto. With his one strong arm he hugged me back and whispered that he just wanted things to go back to what they used to be.

What Dr. Gutierrez and the green guys at the hospital told my mom was that some people who went through what Apá did lost movement in parts of their bodies, sometimes a whole side. They couldn't talk or sometimes think the same.

Maybe it was because Apá loved us so much or because he was so stubborn, but he insisted everything was fine. He said it to all the people who called on the phone too—until the phone stopped ringing. He told us the wheel chair was just for show. He got out of the chair and made a big deal of walking into the living room. He said he felt only a little like he was walking in a bowl of Jello. He said he felt a little slow and sometimes numb, but all he needed was a good stretch. He was almost the same.

Except: the doctors wanted him to take medication. He refused, took up a stretching regimen, doubled up on the garlic and started drinking Chinese herbal tea.

With his second chance also came an avalanche of "no's": no work, no red meat, no salt, no sugar, no cheese, no grease, no smoking, no, no, no. Those "no's" were the hardest part for him. My Amá called them his temptations.

Amá was going to get a job so Apá could stay home and get better. He was passing his business on to his buddy Tomás, at least for a while. Tomás had worked with him for a long time.

Other "no's" were not so easy to control. "Take care of your apá," Amá said. She wanted us to watch out for Apá smoking in the bathroom. She said that we'd know when he did because the one time he'd tried to quit, she'd smelled the smoke on the hand towels. Amá told me to find Apá's cigarettes and hide them.

I found them underneath the bathtub and flushed them down the toilet. Apá didn't say anything about it because that would've been admitting that he was planning on smoking to begin with.

When Apá insisted on driving the few blocks to the grocery store, Amá insisted on a nice walk there instead. She and Clark each grabbed him by one hand so that he had no choice. At the store, they reminded him that he wasn't supposed to eat red meat. He came home with a bag of vegetables and raw dissatisfaction on his face.

Amá grabbed lettuce, tomatoes, onions, cucumbers and limes from the bags. She cut up the vegetables and put them together in an extra-large plastic mixing bowl. She cut a couple of limes in half and squeezed the juice onto the raw veggies. I helped. I opened the refrigerator and put everything away after she was done.

Then she told me to tell Apá that dinner was ready. "Apá!" I yelled out. "Do you want me to get you some salad?"

"I rather have tacos," he answered.

After the salad, we watched a movie. When Silvia forgot to leave the salt off the popcorn, I yelled at her. She yelled back. I never won those shouting matches, but she crumpled when I reminded her it was for my dad.

At bedtime, I looked around. I saw my brothers sucked into the television next to Apá. My dad sat on the couch rubbing his right leg. Silvia stood there with a scowl still on her face. My mom helped my abuelita pack for her return to El Florido. After Abuelita went to sleep, Amá sat on the couch with her head on Apá's shoulder. I saw them like that, and I thought it might be okay.

When I kissed my dad goodnight, he told me how upset he was that we'd been staying home from school, waiting for him. "School is important, mija.

I'm taking you back myself tomorrow," he said. "Now, go to bed." I kissed him goodnight again and again.

Breath

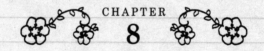

CHAPTER
8

Apá nudged me on the shoulder to get ready for school the next morning. I opened my eyes. He stood there fully dressed in brown pants and the shirt Amá got him the year before when he'd joked it was his 153rd birthday.

I was so relieved to see Apá standing there, I said the first thing that popped into my head—I told him I'd been holding my breath. Apá said it was okay. "I've been catching mine," he said.

Amá kissed us good-bye and wished us luck at school. She was leaving early to drop off job applications so Apá was going to finish getting us ready. Our first day of school outfits had returned to the living room couch. We dressed ourselves once my mom was gone. My special skirt sat on the couch, but I told my dad I didn't want to wear it. He let me wear whatever I wanted. I pulled on a pair of pants that would help me fit into the middle of the week.

Apá let us have sugar cereal for breakfast. We

were usually only allowed to eat sugar cereal on Saturday mornings. "Why is Amá getting a job?" Clark asked Apá with his mouth full.

"She doesn't want to sit at home bored all day with me," Apá told him and laughed at his own joke.

"I'll stay with you," Clark said.

"No, you have to go to school and learn."

Apá hardly ever let us miss school. It was because his father had made him quit young and work hard. It was intense labor, like hauling grain and cleaning pig pens. He wanted us to make the most of the opportunities he'd never had.

Those days Apá was in the hospital were the first time in a long time that we missed school. I'd even gotten a perfect attendance ribbon the year before. Of course, it wasn't always like that. I missed sixty-four days in the first grade. I spent a good part of that year at home with an ear infection and a bad case of *"papí-tis." Papítis* was the word Amá called it when we couldn't bear to spend a single minute away from Apá.

The year I missed that much school, Clark was still a baby. He took up all of Amá's time and Apá took care of the rest of us. If I felt even a little sick, I got up extra early and jumped on top of Apá's mountain of a *pansa*. "Let me go to work with you, Apá," I begged, jumping on his belly, watching it jiggle.

"You know, when I was your age, I wanted to go to school. I loved school. I tramped twenty miles through the snow every day just to get there," he said. I had no idea that it didn't snow like that in Chihuahua.

Still I begged and begged him to let me stay with him. Sometimes he gave in. "Ok. Let's get ready then," he'd say. He'd pull on his work clothes, and I'd put on comfortable clothes. He'd grab his hard hat, and we'd be on our way.

When we got old enough that missing more than a few days of math made a difference in our grades, my dad didn't let us stay home anymore.

When Clark begged to stay with him that first day back in school after his stroke, the answer was a firm NO.

After we ate, Silvia took Clark and me outside. She hissed at us not to bug my dad about staying home anymore. If we kept bugging him or cried, it was only going to make him feel bad. Did we want him to feel bad?

At the front door, Apá checked our backpacks to make sure we had our school supplies. Since Amá had hidden the truck keys, Apá walked us to school. He didn't make Clark ride the little kid bus, but let him walk with us instead. He held his hand the whole way there.

Apá let Silvia and Angel Jr. walk into their school on their own. The middle school was right across the street from the elementary school, and Amá had already called them to explain everything.

It wasn't that easy for Clark and me. Apá walked us to the principal's office. He liked going in and saying hello to everyone when he dropped us off. The ladies there knew him. They also knew about the hospital because Amá had told the principal's secretary, and the office ladies liked to gossip. They told Apá how great it was to have him back.

When Apá hugged Clark good-bye and left, Clark cried. They weren't soft tears. It was full-on bawling. I wanted to cry too. What if my dad wasn't home when we got out? What if something bad happened again? What if this time we weren't there? I was as scared as Clark, but I remembered what Silvia said. I whispered in Clark's ear. I asked him to stop or the office ladies were going to have to call my dad. Then he was going to make my dad feel bad. Clark calmed down, and I walked him the rest of the way to his classroom. Then the bell rang, so I ran to my first day of class.

JUAN
&
ᒋᴇᴄI
IREVER

SOUTHSIDE
BEARS
#1

Small

CHAPTER
9

By the time I actually started sixth grade, I felt like a *burra*—a donkey, which was what they called the kids who weren't too smart. We had missed a little more than a week of school. Nothing was like it was supposed to be. I wasn't sure how to explain it, except that I felt very small.

I was like the new kid even though I'd been at the same school my whole life. I even got the ugly leftover chair. It had a bent-up metal tube that reached into a slab of wood which had probably been attacked by angry woodpeckers. I hung my backpack on the ugly chair and put my notebooks and binder in the rusty basket underneath. I had no choice.

I sat there at the back of class where I couldn't even see the chalkboard. The most I could see of my best friend Nora was the back of her head. I probably wouldn't get to talk to her until lunch.

I became hypnotized by the clock's tick tock, tick tock. "Put your books away now. It's time to go to the cafeteria," the teacher, Ms. Hamlin, finally said. She pulled out her keys and a little plastic bag full of tiny carrots from her desk drawer.

Ms. Hamlin wasn't like any other teacher I'd ever had. She looked like a high school kid. Her hair was short and flipped up at the ends. She wasn't much taller than a sixth grader. She didn't speak Spanish either so she probably hadn't grown up in El Paso. One hour a day, we switched teachers with another class. She taught them Social Studies. Their teacher, Mr. Guerrero, taught us Spanish language, which I already knew perfectly, of course!

When Ms. Hamlin turned off the light, we put our books away and placed our heads on our desks. I sat quiet as a mouse with my head down. I waited for Ms. Hamlin to call out my name. "Miguel, Roy, Aaron...," Miss Hamlin began calling out names. "Ollin, Izcalli, Arturo, Brenda, Antonia, Nora, Camila...," she went on.

Yes, Camila hadn't moved to another school after all. Maybe she'd gotten scared of not knowing anyone at the private school.

My own name drummed in my head, but not in Ms. Hamlin's voice. The real voices grew farther and farther away and the tick tock got louder and louder. I started to think about what my dad might be doing at home. The door jiggled and locked before I knew it. I jumped up out of my chair. Everyone was gone! I tried the door. It was locked from the outside. They'd forgotten me!

I walked to the window and pulled aside the blinds. On the other side of the window was a neat row of new portable classrooms. I returned to my desk. I took out my pencil case and chose the pencil with the biggest eraser. I traced the carvings in front of me, trying to figure out what to do. "Juan & Ceci forever. Southside Bears #1." There were other scribbles from other kids, scratched over and erased. I put my finger in my mouth and wet it. I pressed it against the wood, smearing the marks. I rubbed at the words until they turned into tiny curls of dirt.

My dad was probably eating cardboard for lunch, and just as miserable as me. I stared at the clock and its long arm, tick-tocking from under the light cast by the sun coming through a broken blind. Amazingly, only five minutes had passed.

I heard the door handle turn. I quickly pushed the pencil and case back inside the desk. I stood up straight. I rushed toward the door. "Chela! What are you doing here?" Ms. Hamlin exclaimed. "How did you get here?"

"I never left! You never called my name." I looked at her.

"Oh, Chela, I forgot you started class today. Come on. It's a good thing I came back for my grade book." She grabbed her things and we rushed to the lunchroom. "I'm not sure what happened," she explained. She apologized five times before heading to the teachers' lounge. I didn't say anything. I still wanted her to like me.

When I reached the front of the cafeteria, I saw a man in a hat standing by the door. It couldn't be! It was Apá! I ran to him. "What's going on?" I asked.

"We're going on a picnic," he told me. He had already talked to the office ladies about taking us out of school for lunch. Silvia, Angel Jr. and skinny little Clark waited outside.

We walked out the school's front gate. There was the truck, sitting in front of the little park down the street from the school. He'd searched for the keys all morning and finally found them. He opened the double cab door and pulled out a pair of red and white Whataburger bags. "Waterburger!" Clark squealed.

"Don't worry, I'm only having a grilled chicken sandwich," Apá said when Silvia started in on him about the food and the driving. Sometimes she was pushier than Amá.

Apá winked at me. I sat down next to him on one of the park benches, and smiled a smile bigger than me. I forgot all about my absentminded teacher. I was with my dad, and only that mattered.

CLONES

CHAPTER
10

I finished my class work before anyone else that afternoon, and Ms. Hamlin gave me the okay to use the only computer with the Oregon Trail game on it. It was a game where people pretended they were settlers and crossed a river, got married, wrote their name on the mountains and on just about anything.

Nora came over when she finished her work. There was something different about her as she walked toward me, but I couldn't figure out what. We hadn't been face to face all day. I wanted to tell her about my dad coming home from the hospital and the lunch picnic. We hadn't talked since before he'd gotten sick.

Before I could say anything, Roy, who everyone thought was the cutest boy in school, walked up behind us. He watched the game quietly, waiting for a turn. The three of us were quiet until Nora looked at him and said, "Hey Roy! Chela was just saying she thinks you're cute. She wrote your name on the trail."

I hadn't even opened my mouth, much less about a boy. I didn't understand why she had told him that. My heart fell into my shoe. I made like I hadn't heard. I stared straight ahead, then I stood up and took the bathroom pass. I didn't look at Roy.

I hurried into the girls' bathroom and locked the door. I didn't want to think. I turned on the hand dryer and the water in the sink and left them running. I pushed the lever on the toilet paper dispenser and the paper hand towels until there was nothing left. I didn't even hear the dryer or the water. There was only the pounding of that heart inside my shoe. My foot was pumping gallons of blood straight into my face.

Someone knocked, then jiggled the door handle. "Chela," Ms. Hamlin said. "I need the pass back."

I slid the pass under the door and heard her walk away. Miss Hamlin was young, but she was also old, and couldn't help. When I became so transparent that I disappeared into the bathroom tiles, I opened the door. Nora sat against the wall next to the bathroom. She had on a guilty crooked smile that reminded me of when she lost her sister's favorite sweater.

"Don't smile at me," I told her, throwing a wad of paper at her.

"Don't be mad. The bell rang already," she said. "I was just teasing. Maybe I was mean. Listen, I thought you should know. Camila invited me to be a part of her group at lunch. I don't know why, but she doesn't like you so I can't be your friend anymore. I'm sorry."

She grabbed her book bag and walked away.

I could follow her, but what would I say? I couldn't compete. Camila could make people instantly popular. Anyone who spent time with her got noticed. Everyone knew her, even the teachers. It had always been like that. At first, it was because of her family. Her brother and sister taught at our school. Her cousin was a substitute. Her mom was president of the PTA.

But Camila also came close to being perfect. "How polite" and "how smart" the teachers always said about her. She'd always been an A-class girl and always won the spelling bee. She was possibly the most beautiful sixth grade girl. Her long shiny black hair fell past her waist. She had clothes like only Barbie dolls wore.

Most of the girls in school wanted to be like Camila. Suddenly, I knew what was different about Nora. From a certain angle, she looked like Camila already. Same clothes. Same shoes.

Nora walked toward where Camilla's group hung out after school. She didn't look back. I followed her through the maze of kids still leaving the building until she became just another kid in the crowd. I couldn't imagine that she was the same girl I called best friend for most of my life.

Nora and I'd met in kindergarten. Back then, we were also close friends with Roy and his best friend Miguel. We were friends like only really little kids could be. We rode our bikes together. We went to the corner store together. If the clerk seemed even a little distracted, Miguel and Roy walked in, pretended to look, took penny candy in between their fingers, and made knuckles as they left. Outside, they undid their fists and dropped Hershey's Kisses in our hands.

As soon as we got too old for those trips, Nora and I started watching *telenovelas* after school at my house. *Telenovelas* were Cinderella stories. In *La Fiera*, our favorite, a poor girl met a boy with money, fell in love, was hated by his family, found out she was really rich all along, and—of course— they lived happily ever after.

Nora always wanted to be *in-love* like in the soaps. Once she even had a crush on Miguel, freckles and all. That's when she got it into her head that I should like Roy. Roy had big brown eyes and his last name was Gonzalez too. "If you marry him, you can keep your last name, just like my cousin Irma. For now, you can just kiss him," Nora had told me.

Nora was obsessed with kissing boys ever since she saw her sister making out with her boyfriend. Camila talked about kissing boys all the time too. She and Nora were going to make great friends.

I walked home alone and didn't tell anyone about the bad stuff that happened that day. It nagged at me, but Silvia had said not to worry Apá. Maybe I didn't want to believe it was true either—that Nora meant to embarrass me, that Nora meant to forget about me, that Nora had already forgotten about me.

Hvnger

CHAPTER
11

I decided I hated lunch.

I didn't hate food. I just hated going to the school cafeteria alone.

The very little kids at my school, like Clark, ate lunch inside their classrooms. Maybe they did it that way so they wouldn't get lost, like sheep. I halfway wished our class did that too. Those kids didn't have to worry about who they were going to sit with. They just sat at their regular desks. That's where they drank their milk and ate their chicken nuggets or fought with their teachers about what they didn't want to eat. Then they went back to their classwork.

Older kids ate in the cafeteria, at tables assigned by class, and we had to pick who to sit next to.

At midday the next day, Ms. Hamlin asked us to put our heads down. I hoped that she'd forget me again or that my dad would come back for another picnic. Ms. Hamlin began calling students to stand in line. She called out my name and nodded eagerly when I got my book bag and stood up. It was like she was proud of having remembered me.

I stayed as close to the end of the line as possible. I imagined ducking into the bathroom and hiding so I didn't have to sit alone. I'd have no one to sit with since Nora had traded me in. I clutched my book bag close to my chest and hoped that catching up on the work I'd missed while I ate would help me not look or feel so alone. I wasn't sure how I was going to get through lunch period that day.

Ms. Hamlin walked us to the counter and watched us load our trays with meatloaf, milk and juice boxes. She guided us to our table. When another teacher walked by, they started talking.

Nora was already sitting with Camila, Brenda, and Toña. She'd stopped wearing her glasses. She picked at her food and her naked eyes avoided me. "It would be terrible to have no friends. I'm glad we all have each other," Camila said as I walked by.

Nora and I used to have each other.

Nora had said she didn't know why Camila disliked me. I didn't understand either, but Camila hated me so much that she'd taken my best friend. She already had her group. Brenda and Toña, the other two girls she was always with, were carbon copies of their leader. They were like all the other girls in our school who wanted to be like Camila, but Brenda and Toña had known Camila longer and better. They came closer to being like her than anyone else with their long hair and Barbie clothes.

Now Nora was one of them too. She had mutated into a popular girl.

I sat alone at the faraway end of the table. I tried to eat, but my tongue was dry and unwilling to push anything down. I sipped my juice and tossed the rest of the food away.

All of the other kids in my grade ran out into the school yard as soon as they finished eating. I looked out past the double row of windows that reached up to the cafeteria's ceiling. The boys played kickball or marbles.

The girls sat around in groups and talked. Maybe they talked about which boys they liked this year. I didn't go out there. I sat in the cafeteria and worked on my math word problems until the bell rang.

Catching up on the homework I missed those first weeks of school wasn't hard. I concentrated more on my work than ever before. I had no one to distract me, during lunch or any time. I had no one to whisper to in class or to sit with and trade notes. I didn't have anyone to walk home with either.

That's why I decided to wait outside of Silvia's school and follow her home. She was with one of her friends and pretty annoyed that I was hanging around. She walked very fast and a few steps in front of me, like she didn't know me.

I might as well have walked home alone. That's exactly what I'd go back to doing the next day.

My dad asked us how school went. I smiled and tried to say as little as possible without lying. I told him they served meatloaf, and carefully avoided saying I had eaten it. "But I'm still hungry," I added.

Apá had lost a few pounds at the hospital and told me he could relate. There was a lot of home cooking he couldn't eat anymore so he always felt hungry. "I miss the *mole,* enchiladas, gorditas, chiles rellenos and menudo," he said. He missed all the spicy sauces, fried foods, and forbidden pork.

"When I first came to the United States," he told me, "I was barely older than Angel Jr. I traveled all over the Southwest and lived in half a dozen *pueblitos* before getting out to California where your aunt lived. Some of those towns had never even seen a burrito. They served up salted sliced meat, white bread, and unbuttered mashed potatoes runny with water. I'd never seen food like that, and I was afraid to eat it. I walked around on empty. Eventually, I got hungry enough that I had no choice but to eat it. Eventually, even food you don't like satisfies you."

That wasn't exactly what I had meant. I didn't mind the cafeteria food.

"Oh, meatloaf isn't so bad," I told him. "Besides, my teacher says eating makes you taller." Of course, what she'd said was that we needed to eat because we were growing.

"Okay, I always believe a teacher. Let's make you something," he said. We walked into the kitchen. I stood up next to him and measured with my hand how I reached up to his chin. I was almost as tall as Silvia. "You'll see. I'll be your size by the time we finish eating," I said. We laughed.

Apá and I sat and talked about all the things they were teaching in sixth grade. There were ratios, volume, areas, animal cells, Confucius and the Greek gods. Meanwhile, he made me a strawberry *licuado*. We chugged the cold strawberry smoothies. It wasn't exactly enchiladas or gorditas, but after that I didn't feel so empty.

AmeriCa

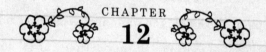

CHAPTER
12

Amá made dinner and an announcement. Her friend had offered her a job at a place taking care of old people. Apá asked her if it was something like what she did with him. "You're not old!" she told him.

My mom married my father when she was nineteen and he was thirty. She'd never worked a job outside of being the boss of our home. "I know you don't want me to work, but we have things to pay. I want to help," Amá said.

Then Apá made his own announcement. Mrs. Ortega, one of his oldest clients, was paying him money that she owed him with land. Apá said that he was going to sell part of it and build a house for us on the other part. The lot of land was only two blocks from the house we were renting—the house that wasn't ours.

"You're not well enough to work on something like that," Amá told him. But my father declared he was never one to live or die by someone else's predictions.

"I'm not dead yet," he told her. "You would have

me be one of those *viejitos* you're going to take care of. This is something that I should've done long ago when we had all the time in the world. This was what we always planned. This is why we decided to stay here. I can do this."

What he meant was that it was the reason they had put in the paperwork to become American citizens. I didn't understand it when they first told us about American citizenship. Maybe nothing would really change. We already lit firecrackers on the Fourth of July and barbequed our *carne asada*.

Before the paperwork, when the *migra* told Apá that he wasn't allowed to be someplace and asked him his citizenship, he was already telling them, American. To Apá, that wasn't a lie. It wasn't a lie to ever call himself American because the Americas were two continents.

"I was born on one of them," he said. "Besides, Texas used to be part of Mexico." I didn't blame the border patrol guy for not knowing. Up until the first day of kindergarten when they taught us the Pledge of Allegiance, I thought Texas was still just a part of Mexico.

One of the first things Apá found out when he settled in El Paso was that almost everyone was Mexican, so people couldn't tease you about that, about being Mexican. The thing they would tease you about was being born on the other side. People born in Juarez were like third graders, maybe worse. People born in the U.S. were like sixth graders. They felt bigger and more important, so they bullied the third graders.

Being born on the other side didn't make Apá feel ashamed or wish he were born in the United States. That wasn't why he eventually became a citizen. He didn't want us to be ashamed that he had come from El Florido and then crossed through Juarez, either. He made it a point to help us be proud no matter what. He taught us about Mexican role models like Benito Juarez, Mexico's greatest president. He wanted us to know as much about him as we did about George Washington.

The Mexican city across the border was named after President Juarez. The only other person who ever taught us about that was my second-grade teacher, Ms. Juarez. Whenever our class let out, the other classes yelled, "Here come the kids from Juarez!" They also called us Juareños, which was an insult. They called us Juareños like they were calling us dogs. "The right word for people from Juarez is Juarenses," my dad said.

When our second-grade teacher overheard kids making fun of Juarez and making fun of her name too, she told us to not pay attention. She told us about how Juarez was a hero. "He fought for Mexico's independence from France. He fought for equal rights for everyone, better doctors and schools. He also did a lot to help the poor," she said.

I already knew about Juarez because of my dad. Juarez had been born the son of full-blooded Zapotec

Indians. His parents had died when he was a baby. He had grown up poor, and his life had been tough. But he hadn't given up. He'd gone on to become president of his country.

Sometimes Ms. Juarez asked us to think about nice memories of Ciudad Juarez, because everyone living in El Paso had been there or at least visited. We drew pictures of whatever we thought up, and she put happy face stickers on our work. Sometimes I drew pictures of my dad buying us pistachio ice cream pops or fresh-made corn tortillas rolled up with salt. Sometimes I drew a picture of visiting my tías Tere and Belen, my mom's sisters, who lived there now.

The night of the big announcements, I sat down next to Apá after dinner and asked him if he missed pistachio ice cream pops. "We'll go to Juarez soon and have a cone, *mija*," my dad said.

My mom scolded me when my dad left the room. She told me not to eat bread in front of the poor. I told her that I only ate what she gave me and that I was done eating. She said she meant I shouldn't talk to my dad about pistachio ice cream and make him want things he couldn't have. In a loud whisper, my mom reminded me that my dad wasn't exactly the same.

But Apá was trying hard to prove he was the same. That night, I listened to him setting up his work table outside. I heard the conversation he had with his table saw. He stood out there with his thick waist leaned up against his table, his newly grown peppered beard lost in the smoke of a secret cigarette. He sang his heartbroken Pedro Infante song. That was how Apá started building our house.

Chiple

CHAPTER
13

Apá offered to take me to the library the following weekend. It was one of his favorite places, and it would give me something to do. I'd caught up on my school work in just a few days, and the daily assignments went by so fast that missing Nora was getting harder and harder. I still wanted to talk to her, but she wouldn't even look at me. Camila ruled 6-A. No girl in class would get close to me unless Camila did. She might take away their friends too.

I'd had plenty of friends the year before. Angelica, Bianca, Clarissa, Yaretzi, Nora and I made fun of the 5-A girls behind their backs when we were in 5-B. We played soccer, basketball, and kickball together in PE class. We also ate lunch together and hung out for a few minutes after school talking about our homework.

I wasn't sure why we weren't friends anymore, but people from different classes never really hung out with each other at school. It might've been different if any of them lived near me, because then we might've spent time together after school. But all of those girls lived on the other side of the Cotton Street Bridge. I wasn't allowed to wander that way by myself.

I needed to find something else to do with my free time, so I found a book in the kid's section of Armijo Library that looked like it was three hundred pages long. It was probably the fattest book there. It didn't have pictures inside or on the cover. It didn't have a book jacket. The librarian, a broom of a lady, looked at it with a raised eyebrow when I checked it out. Right before she scanned it, she told me the book was too "big" for me. Never mind that I found it in the kid's section.

I took it from the counter and didn't say anything. I sat down in their reading room with my dad and tried it for a while. It wasn't easy to read, but I grabbed a dictionary and copied the words I didn't know and wanted to understand. It was a sad story about an immigrant girl during the time of the pioneers.

When I got home, I carried the book and our house dictionary with me to the living room, then to my bed that night. I read it with a flashlight underneath my blankets.

That night the universe was dark, even with a sliver of moon and my small beam. I read until my heavy eyelids pulled me somewhere else. I was halfway finished when I carried it into the bathroom in the morning to brush my teeth. I walked with it in one hand and my toothbrush in the other.

"Reading is good. That book can be your new best friend," Apá said.

"That's for sure. She has no other friends," Silvia told him and laughed.

Of course, he had no idea. He knew I'd been sitting around the house a lot, but I hadn't told him about Nora. Silvia was the one who had ordered us not to worry him, but Silvia was careless with the truth.

"That's none of your business," I told her with a mouth full of toothpaste. I pushed past her to spit in the sink. I walked back to the living room fully dressed. My dad stopped me and asked if I was okay.

I needed to talk to someone so I finally told Apá that the girls at school hated me. I told him Silvia was right. I told him I felt like those dogs at the pound we saw that time that he, Silvia and I went there. All those orphan eyes said, "Pick me." With hot tears welling up in my eyes, I told him I wanted someone to hurry up and pick me.

"I pick you," Apá told me and squeezed my shoulder as if we were going into a soccer game. He smiled. Some people might think it was a lame thing for him to say, but he'd lifted something dark and heavy that'd been pushing me down. Then I smiled back. I hugged him and tried to get my short arms around his entire belly. I told him I loved him.

Apá went to get dressed. When I heard him come near the door, I rubbed my ear and said, "Apá, I have an earache." I wanted him to remember how he let me miss school when I was very little. I wanted him to say I could stay home and go help him with our new house. With an occasional helping hand from Tomás, he worked on the house all day until we came home from school. Then he watched us in the afternoon until Amá got home from her new job.

I complained about my ear, but Amá heard first. She snapped at me for always being *chiple* with my dad.

We did act pretty spoiled. She made sure my dad wasn't listening and went in for the kill. "If it hurts that much, I'll let you miss one day of school," she said. "We'll put some Vicks on a cotton ball inside your ear. You can lie in bed all day. But don't even THINK about bothering your apá. He can't be worrying about you. Go bring me the Vicks from the cabinet in the bathroom."

She pulled a Silvia on me and made me feel guilty. I took the cotton ball, got dressed, picked up my fat book, and followed Silvia to school. I didn't want to bother Apá.

The Street

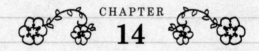

CHAPTER
14

After school, Silvia asked Apá if she could *dar una vuelta a la manzana*—take a walk. He gave her permission with the condition that she take me.

The only way my parents would let either of us go anywhere other than school and farther than three blocks was to take each other. She was only going down the street this time, but it was Apá's way of teaching her a lesson for being mean to me that morning.

"You need to learn to get along," Apá told her.

"Put on your shoes and let's go," Silvia snapped when she walked into our room. Then, when she looked over her back and saw that Apá was still watching, she smiled plastic and even helped me find my shoes.

We walked past the old-people apartments and the San Jacinto building that used to be a school. We walked two blocks in the direction of the Dairy Queen. A giant red billboard, with pinned-on numbers and letters, announced banana splits on special for ninety-nine cents.

My mouth watered. We never went there. The only ice cream we ate out was the pistachio in Juarez. If we wanted banana splits, we made them ourselves with ice cream from the grocery store gallon tub, bananas, chocolate syrup and strawberry marmalade.

We walked into the Dairy Queen, and Silvia pulled out her *monedero*. She pushed her face down close to the coin wallet in her palm. She put on her sometimes-glasses, counted, and quickly took them off when she was done. She slapped a dollar in dimes on the counter.

"I only have enough for one," she told me. "We're gonna share."

I thought her sharing meant maybe we might start doing more things together. Maybe she actually did feel guilty about being bossy and making fun of me. But I had a dollar too. I pulled the bill from the back pocket of my jeans and showed her.

Silvia gave me a look like where did I get that

from. I told her I'd taken it from my piggy bank. I didn't actually have a piggy bank so much as an old mayonnaise jar in my underpants drawer where I kept the almost nine dollars I'd saved up. Silvia shrugged and put her wallet away.

We sat in a booth that faced the large glass doors. We dug our spoons in. That's when I saw him. A junior-high boy walked into the Dairy Queen. I could tell he was in junior high because he wore one of those green uniform T-shirts from their baseball team.

Silvia nudged me with her elbow. I curled my lips up to make an ugly face at her. I wasn't a good chaperone, so I did exactly as she hinted. I made like a banana and split.

The junior-high boy went by Silvia, sat down, and started flirting before I even got out the door. I guess she'd known he was coming all along.

I walked to the curb and sat down on the pavement. The air outside was just cool enough to keep my ice cream from turning into milk. I lapped it up, watching the buses go by.

I daydreamed about getting on a bus and just going wherever it went. Never mind that I wasn't allowed to ride the bus by myself. I could ride the school bus alone when I was younger, but that was different.

"I don't like you getting on the public bus with all the *locos*," Apá had said. Being a bus driver was one of his many jobs before he'd started working on houses, and he knew about crazies.

We saw a stringy-haired woman barking and biting at her shoulder at a downtown bus stop once. "That's who you might be sitting next to," he told us.

My parents thought I was too young. That was always the reason why I couldn't or shouldn't do something.

I started to think about places I might go. I might go where La Güera went—she was one of our cousins from El Florido who used to clean houses on the Westside where the rich people lived. We called her that because she looked like a white girl—big pink friendly face, blue eyes and blondish hair just like all those California girls on the magazine covers. Except that when she opened her mouth, perfect Spanish spilled out. One day La Güera decided to move to Los Angeles and become a real California girl.

I wanted to go someplace like that. And why not? My parents hadn't always lived in El Paso. They'd moved here, and one day I might move someplace far away too. I'd go to a new school and make new friends.

I guess if I'd said that to them, they'd have told me they were older then, and I was too young to be thinking like that. But I just wanted a whole new life.

Out Loud

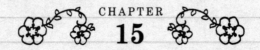

CHAPTER
15

I didn't move far away, but I kept daydreaming about it—especially on the morning that we read about Athena.

In my fifth grade bilingual class everyone spoke funny like me. But kids who'd been in the A-classes since kindergarten were different. They spoke mostly English at home and sounded a lot like the people on television. I'd never read out loud in front of kids like that.

I was nervous, so I sped up and stumbled over myself. I read: "A-ra-q-knee said that she could weave the most beautiful tap-tape-estry. This made Athena angry and terrible."

In that instant Camila's group went from pretending I didn't exist to snickering behind my back. "Chelota is a Juareñota. Chelota is a Juareñota," Camila chimed under her breath and laughed. I could tell by the look on Nora's face that she didn't want to join them, but she wasn't defending me either. It was the kind of thing that made other kids cry, but I ground my teeth until they made a noiseless sound that rang in my ears.

A normal teacher would've said something to them. All Ms. Hamlin said was, "Eyes on the book, girls." It probably wasn't that she didn't care. Her head was just always in the clouds. And, since she hadn't grown up in El Paso, she didn't understand what an insult being called a Juareña was.

Ms. Hamlin asked me to try again. My words were hesitant and rough, a tight attack on the air, a punch, sharp thuds. "Arachne said that she could weave the most beautiful tape-estry. This made Athena angry and terrible," I repeated.

I didn't understand. I could read perfectly in my head. My enemies, who spoke a seamless English, continued to giggle.

"What's a tapestry?" Ms. Hamlin interrupted. The enemies looked at me expectantly. It was almost like Ms. Hamlin was making fun of my reading too, of my "tape-estry." But she wasn't. She just wanted the definition.

She turned to all of us and asked, "Can anyone

describe what a tapestry is?" I quickly raised my hand. It was an easy word.

"Chela. Go ahead," Ms. Hamlin pointed to me.

"It's a *tapicería*!" I said, my Spanish oozing out. Camila and her clones burst into another set of mean giggles.

I couldn't help it. I'd learned to speak Spanish before I'd learned English. El Segundo Barrio ran along the Mexican border, and that's how it was for a lot of kids in my neighborhood. I'd formed my definitions from staying up with Apá watching old cowboy movies. He always forgot his glasses on purpose and made me read the subtitles out loud. Thanks to John Wayne and my father's infinite wisdom, I'd learned that letters formed words and that for almost everything in English there was something in Spanish. It also worked the other way around.

I heard their giggling, and I wanted to kick myself for thinking in Spanish and answering in translation. I wasn't ashamed of the way I learned things or the way I spoke, but I didn't like being laughed at.

"Before we close our books, tell me what a tap-ee-cerea is," Ms. Hamlin said. I scrolled inside my head for an English answer. The enemy girls twisted their smiles and rolled their eyes. They maybe thought that I didn't know.

"A *tapicería* is a decorative woven cloth with designs," I finally said.

"Very good!" Ms. Hamlin exclaimed.

As we left for lunch, Ms. Hamlin tapped me on the shoulder and told me to come in from lunch five minutes early because she wanted to talk to me. I wasn't sure what she wanted to talk about, but some of the boys in class teased me and went *OOOOOOOOOH* like they liked to do when someone got in trouble.

All through lunch, I pretended to read my book and wondered what she wanted to talk about. Maybe she wanted me to congratulate her for having remembered I was around this whole time. Maybe she wanted to ask me why I always ate lunch alone. Maybe she HAD noticed how mean the other girls were to me. Whatever it was, I was okay with it because it meant five less minutes of sixth grade lunch torture.

It was none of the things I turned around in my head. Ms. Hamlin wanted to sign me up to take a special test to get into the Gifted and Talented program. It was the first time our school was offering the program. In the past, kids who wanted to participate had to move to another school. Also, since it was new, it would only meet after the school bell on Wednesdays. GT projects included writing poetry and creating science experiments.

I told Ms. Hamlin that I'd talk to my parents about it. I knew that I'd either make new friends in GT or add another couple of hours of suffering to my week.

The program sounded like fun even with no friends. I felt very proud of myself for the rest of the day. I held my head up whenever I walked by the enemy group.

Smart

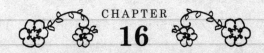

CHAPTER
16

On Saturday morning, a couple of weeks after taking the GT test, I spent the day in Juarez with my family. It was our first visit across the border since my dad had gotten sick. We were going to a *kermes*. Church block parties had rides, games, shows and food.

I showered quickly and put on my favorite outfit—a pair of green slacks and a short-sleeved white shirt with silver button snaps and frogs embroidered on it. My dad wore nice clothes and his going-out hat, one like the golfers wore.

"I don't want to get sunburned," he joked as he put it on. The sun was out, but it wasn't hot. It was a perfect day to be outside.

At the *kermes*, my parents said hello to all kinds of people they knew, people that us kids couldn't really remember ever seeing. We politely said hello as we walked by. We walked past stands of pork tacos and shredded beef gorditas with lots of chile, cilantro and onions. My mouth watered.

Before I begged my dad for anything, my mom reminded us we'd already eaten and hissed at us not to ask. She'd put us all on his new diet.

My dad played the deaf guy. He ordered each of us steaming hot cups of *elote*. White corn was exactly what I wanted—drowned in Valentina sauce, lime juice and grated cheese.

A man from a nearby dart-throwing booth called Apá over while we waited. Apá aimed and quickly won a box of tequila lollipops, the kind with the worms in them. We dug into the corn. Once the last empty styrofoam cup bounced off the rim of the trashcan and dropped inside, my dad sat with Amá by a tree. He peeled dollar bills from his wallet and handed one over to each of us. Angel Jr. took Clark by the hand and headed straight for the arcade games. My sister and I traded our money for ten tickets to the aluminum tilt-a-whirl. It was the closest I'd ever been to flying, and we stayed on until we ran out of tickets.

Silvia's plan was to ask for more money when we walked back to the tree. I couldn't wait to get back on, but a sharp claw closed around my belly. "I think the ride made my *pansa* hurt," I said to Silvia.

"Ok, see ya," Silvia answered and headed out with the extra dollar from my dad. The claw loosened its grip, but I didn't feel better. It felt like when you eat too much candy or put too much chile on your potato chips.

"I told you not to buy them junk. It was probably the corn," my mom told my dad. "She's not having any ice-cream pops later. No one is."

"No! Amá, don't be ugly," I burst out.

"*¡Ey!* Don't talk like that to your mother!" Apá scolded me. I stood there with my mouth open until my dad called me to sit down next to them. My mom was being mean, and my dad was taking her side.

I sat on a neighboring bench making angry fish faces. Amá and Apá ignored me. Apá gave Amá little kisses so she wouldn't be mad at him for buying the junk food. It made me even more nauseous. I didn't want to see them be mushy. I tried to think of a million other things until the sun got too lazy to hold itself up and the ticket seller told us it was time to go home.

Everyone was upset about not having ice cream before leaving, but my dad took the blame and said it was because he wouldn't be able to resist it if he saw us eating. Angel Jr. must've suspected it was my fault because the whole ride home, he shot at me with spit and made it seem like the bullets came from his nose. He picked his nose with one finger, grabbed spit with the other and pointed at me.

When we got home, I stood behind Amá. She unlocked the door too slowly. I stomped up the stairs. After a few minutes, I heard footsteps. There was a knock and then my dad. He held a letter from the school district's main office. It'd been sitting in the mailbox.

Then I realized my stomach had stopped churning and there were butterflies. I forgot all about being sore. My dad tore open the letter while I held my breath. He read out loud: "Your daughter has tested gifted and is being offered placement in our new after-school program."

All they had to do was sign the permission slip. Apá wasn't surprised. "See! You're smart. I told you all you had to do was work hard," he said.

It wasn't that I was conceited, but I did feel smart. The letter said I was "gifted." My dad was proud, and he read it out loud again during our salad dinner. Angel Jr. repeated it just like that; he said "gifted" in quotation marks. Then he reminded me that when I was four, I thought corn came from the closet. Never mind that the kind of corn Amá made at home did come from the closet.

After that day, the minutes no longer dragged into days and weeks. Everything went by fast.

friend

CHAPTER
17

Camila, Brenda and Toña were in the GT program—no one else. They only talked to me when the teacher made us work together or to poke fun at me. It made me want to ask my dad to take back the permission slip, but that wouldn't have been fair. I liked what we were learning.

I overheard Camila and her clones talking about how only Brenda, who spoke baby Spanish in language class, actually tested gifted. Camila and Toña hadn't passed, but the school couldn't start a Gifted and Talented program with only two people, so they added the kids with the top grades in the A-class the previous year.

Nora wasn't in. She hadn't passed the test or been in the A-class the year before.

During the first six weeks of GT, we designed a food dehydrator, videotaped a commercial, planned original science experiments, and had a powwow. Still, there were some things that were more work than fun. Like: drawing out a ten-thousand-year timeline.

Then there was the poetry writing. In the bathroom, Brenda and Toña whispered how Camila copied her poems from a magazine and turned them in as hers because she couldn't find her own words. They never snitched on her. I never snitched on them. I didn't want them to get back at me for it. Maybe I just couldn't find the words to speak up.

I walked home alone from GT every week. Of course I walked home alone even on the other days of the week, but at least there were lots of other kids around then.

One afternoon, as I walked home from GT, I heard the sound of someone following behind me— it was the squeal of bicycle wheels a block outside of school. I was a little jumpy and looked over my shoulder. That's how I found myself staring into a pair of big brown eyes.

"Roy?" Roy got off his bicycle and walked beside me rolling his bike along.

"I stayed late for tutoring," he said as he adjusted his backpack with one hand. "I can give you a ride," he laughed nervously. I laughed a little nervously too.

"You like walking alone?" he asked.

"It's not horrible."

"I walk home alone after tutoring too. Maybe we can walk home together sometimes," he said. I was mute for a second. Then I nodded my head. I mumbled something about it being nice. He winked as he mounted his bike. He zoomed away. It was the first time we'd talked since Nora had stabbed me in the back.

When Apá came home from working on the new house, we sat in front of the television watching a telenovela I sort of liked. It was probably all the kissing on TV that made me ask him, "How did you and Amá fall in love?"

He told me he still had all his hair when he met my mom. Since he was an orphan, her family took pity on him and let him sleep in their barn and share their dinner. It was Amá's job to call him to the table every night. She was only four years old.

"Mari was a skinny annoying little kid with freckles and braids. I moved away soon after that, and we didn't see each other for many years. Your amá spent that time growing up and becoming beautiful."

"You fell in love when you saw her again?" I asked.

"When I saw her again, she was the most beautiful girl I'd ever laid eyes on. The freckles and braids were gone. A lot changed about her, but never her eyes. They were still the same dark sparkling eyes," he said. "We got married soon after that."

It was a great story and it was very romantic because it had actually happened.

I didn't like Roy in that way or the way they did in the soap operas, but I remembered him being a nice friend, and I needed those. Roy smiled and said hello to me in class from that day on. Other kids in our class started smiling too, but they didn't come too close. The Camila group still turned their noses up and laughed behind my back or ignored me. I didn't mind that so much because being ignored was better than being picked on.

I don't know why any of it was so, but it was.

Roy and I walked home together on the days when we both stayed late. He rode his bike and played sports with his brother and friends on the other days.

Sometimes Roy and I studied together. He told me he liked studying with me because I always coughed up the right answers when the teacher called on me in class. It also impressed him that I was in the after-school program and got straight A's on my last report card.

"I could tell you were smart even before you were in my class. I'd see you carrying all your books in the morning," he said to me. He smiled shyly, and I wasn't sure if he was joking.

When he came over to my house, we did homework on the back porch. We sat on my dad's log bench. We didn't study together in class because sixth grade boys and girls just didn't do that unless they wanted to be teased.

My whole family teased us enough as it was. My dad even called him my boyfriend. Thankfully, he didn't do it in front of Roy.

Roy was a nice friend, but there were still some things that I just couldn't tell him. I didn't understand a whole lot about boys, and I was sure they didn't understand a whole lot about me.

It was sort of like when school started and Angel Jr. gave me advice when all I really wanted was for Silvia to tell me what she thought.

So Roy and I never talked about how he was my only real school friend.

Shhshs

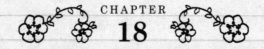

CHAPTER
18

I had only a few chances to talk to kids from other classes. When we lined up to go back to class after PE, a pair of girls who called themselves *cholas*, wore lipstick, and kissed boys behind the portables, marched up and down the girl lines like drill sergeants and talked about stuff that mostly made me squirm.

Betty and Shorty carried an invisible checklist and asked the big question: "What size bra do YOU wear?"

They talked to me more than the people in my own class did, but it wasn't like we were friends. That'd have meant letting them see under my shirt and joining their gang. It'd have meant inviting them to my house, and having my mom find out. It'd have meant giving my mom a reason to take off her *chancla*. My pants hurt at the thought of her shoe stamped on my behind for hanging out with girls who claimed to be gang members. Never mind that these girls mostly just pretended to be tough by wearing lots of eyeliner and talking loud.

Betty, Shorty and everyone else became obsessed with bras right after the PE coach showed us that video about our bodies changing. For the second year in a row, we watched a mother and daughter talking about "the changes" while they made pancakes.

I started feeling like one of those bugs inside a jumping bean. There was nowhere to run. One or two girls started to fidget in their seats and said they actually talked to their mothers about that. That same day, school turned into "Everything you ever wondered about—shhh you can't say those things out loud!" as told by the sixth grade girls.

I didn't tell any of them about my bra or that insane itch under my shirt. I didn't tell the *cholas* that the summer before, my amá came home from her day of paying bills with a present for me.

"I got a surprise for you," she said. *"Son copas."* Cups? I thought she was talking about a tea set. And, even though I was already eleven by then, I was excited. Only, when Amá opened her bag, she pulled out a bra. I never let on what I really expected. Only Nora knew.

After the thing with the "cups," I told Amá to give all of my tight-fitting T-shirts to my younger cousins. I only wore baggy T-shirts and jeans. I wasn't coming out of my shirts or anything, but I was more visible than girls like Nora and Camila. I hated thinking that someone might notice.

It made me remember this girl I knew when I was four named Heather. Heather was four too. She came from Nebraska and the dry heat just about did her in. The days the sun shone so bright the birds would fall from the sky, Heather ripped off her shirt and ran around like the boys. She wasn't embarrassed. When I told my mom, she got mad at me and told me I couldn't play with Heather anymore.

"Only *cochinas* take off their shirts! Pigs!" she said.

When Betty and Shorty came up to me in the PE line and asked about my bra, I hugged my arms tight around my chest. I wondered what would happen if I just took a deep breath, acted like I was looking for something in my backpack and never looked up. I could count my pens and pencils and ignore them.

Their questions embarrassed me, and I wasn't even scared that Shorty might turn red and ask me to meet her in the alley after school to fight me for not answering.

Of course, I never turned the other way, and Shorty never beat me up. I was nice to anyone who talked to me. That's the way my dad had taught us to be. But it was getting harder and harder to cover up what I was hiding.

The day my sister invited me to go swimming with her at Armijo Park's heated pool, I almost said no. I was terrified of walking around in a wet swimsuit. Amá and Apá wouldn't let Silvia go by herself, so she begged. I said yes, only because I wanted her to like me like when we were kids.

I just had to find something to wear that wouldn't

reveal my secrets. I tried on a bunch of things and left a mess of clothes all over my bed. I chose a dark shirt and shorts. I planned to keep them on over my swimsuit even when I jumped in the water.

On Saturday morning, Apá gave us a ride to the swimming pool. Camila was there with Brenda. She wore the same bathing suit I wore, but no cover-up. She wasn't the type to hide. Besides, her body hadn't changed. She pretended not to see me, and I did the same.

I stayed close to Silvia's side when we got in the pool. Two junior-high boys from Silvia's school swam up next to us. I recognized one of them from the Dairy Queen. He started talking to Silvia. I'd never seen the other one before.

"Are you one of Silvia's new friends?" the other boy asked while he treaded water next to me. He had curly hair, and his green eyes stared straight at my chest.

"No."

"The water is deep over there. You want to swim with me?" He smiled with all his teeth.

"No. I have to go," I told him. I didn't stick around long enough to hear him say anything else. I swam even closer to Silvia. She was leaning up against the edge, waiting for the boy from the Dairy Queen to make his move. I nudged her.

"What's wrong? What's up with you?" Silvia asked.

"He was looking at me funny," I told her, and pointed at the green-eyed boy. Silvia turned and told him that he was a pervert and that he better leave me alone, or she was going to tell Angel Jr.

I knew she didn't want me getting down and wanting to go home. She'd have to go home too. The boy from the Dairy Queen went over to talk to his friend and came back telling us how sorry he was that his buddy was such a goober. He flirted with Silvia a little, and I could tell she forgot all about the friend.

"Just ignore him," she said.

We swam until they closed the pool. We didn't bother taking off our wet clothes. We just pulled our sweats over them. It was getting dark so we hurried home. I opened the front door and walked straight up the stairs, leaving invisible chlorine footprints behind.

I stood in front of the mirror. My clothes were still damp and clung even after the walk home. The PE coach told us that growing out of our bodies wouldn't be so bad. She lied. For me it was hard enough being the odd one out without changing bodies at the same time. I was some sort of ugly caterpillar turning into an even uglier moth. I prayed quietly for my chest to stop mutating, at least until Camila's started doing something. Everyone looked up to her even if she'd stolen my best friend. Camila was built like a *tamal*, and maybe secretly prayed her own "shhhhs" would grow in.

When Camila finally got a bra, she made sure she was the first one in line for Betty and Shorty's inspection. She told the story over and over again about her sister taking her to Penney's. She ran off the list of how many colors and kinds of "brassieres" they bought. It was practically on the morning announcements. Everyone unlucky enough to listen quickly became desperate to move on to the next thing.

By the end of two weeks, even she and her clones were bored with it. Then the talking about the other things that happen only to girls got louder.

Ketchup

Even though my mom had gotten me those "cups," we didn't talk about any of those things at home—bodies, bras, or boys. We just avoided them, even when they were looking us straight in the face, waiting.

Take the first time I really paid attention to one of those commercials for lady products on TV. I imagined it was for something good. The women in the ad wore white robes and danced to flute music as if they hadn't a worry in the world. We sat on the living room couch watching it, and I asked Silvia and my cousin Mary why the women seemed so happy. They looked at each other and laughed. It wasn't a cruel laugh. It was uncomfortable like when someone tells a joke that's not funny.

They laughed because they didn't know what else to do. They didn't explain to me what they were selling in the commercial. All they said was, "You don't need to think about that yet." So I never asked again. When I finally did find out, it was at school when we saw the video in PE class.

Not too long after that, I found Clark sitting in front of the bathroom sink with his dwarf back to the door. His skinny little head was inspecting something. The cabinet under the sink was wide open, and there was a blue cardboard box on the linoleum tile whose label I couldn't make out.

I snuck up close enough to lean over him and peek. Like a good spy, I held my breath, and my feet almost floated above the ground as I tiptoed. He didn't see or hear me.

There was a pile of pink on the floor. He held a soft pink plastic pouch in his hand. He unwrapped it, making all that noise that plastic makes. He brought it up to his nose. He looked it over and sniffed at it.

"Silvia!" I yelled to my sister, breaking him out of his spell. He gave me an angry look but didn't stop what he was doing.

Silvia walked in, and her jaw dropped open as if that would make the words come out. I just shook my head from side to side. She looked at me as if asking why I hadn't stopped him from making that huge mess in the first place.

"I just got here," I said. She reached over him and snatched the blue box from him.

"Hey! That's mine," he screamed.

"It's not yours!" she screamed back.

"Yes. I found them."

"No. They're not yours."

"Well, are they yours?" he asked her mockingly.

The blood rushed to her face, and she took a deep breath. "They're our abuelita's diapers. Stop playing with them," she hissed.

She returned a few unopened pink pouches to their place. She picked up the rest and chucked them into the trash can. She closed the box up and pushed it far back into the cabinet. She closed the cabinet door.

That's when Amá walked in to see what all the yelling was about. Amá saw what Clark had in his hand. I pointed to the trash can, so she could see there was more where that came from. She inspected the rest of the bathroom.

"Did you open them all?" Amá asked.

"Yes. The other day you told me they were cookies," he answered. "I was looking for the cookies."

"Since when do we hide cookies in the bathroom? Do we also keep milk in the toilet tank? Boy, you'll believe anything," Silvia said.

"She told me they're diapers. Are these really diapers?" he asked Amá, ignoring Silvia. He still held the one pad. He quickly dropped it on the floor as if someone had peed on it.

"No, those are napkins," Amá told him honestly. She meant sanitary napkins. That's what they'd called them in her time.

Clark didn't know what Amá meant by napkins. I pictured him, age sixteen. He's sitting at the movies with a girl on their first date. He eats a movie-theater hotdog and fries. Ketchup dribbles down his chin. He pulls a maxi pad out of her purse and wipes the ketchup off his face.

I only hoped he'd watch that video at school before anything like that happened.

"Just wait until I tell your father," Amá said.

Apá'd been working on the new house. No one told him anything though, probably because we were all too embarrassed. I don't know what my dad would have done, but I turned red just thinking about it.

I must've been walking home from school when "it" finally happened to me. I got home, and there it was. I didn't tell anyone—not Amá, not my sister, not any of the *cholas* at school, and not the girl who had been my best friend.

I wondered if Nora had gotten it yet. Other girls wished for it to happen. Some of them changed when it did. They cared about different things. I hoped I hadn't transformed in any way people could tell.

But just like I said nothing to anyone, no one said anything to me.

The World

CHAPTER
20

The morning of our Christmas party, the desk aisles doubled as fashion runways for the enemy girls to show off their holiday clothes. I rolled my eyes, followed the boys, and walked the other way. Ms. Hamlin had cleared a space for all the goodies in our snack potluck. I placed my three-liter orange soda on the window shelf with the other drinks, cookies, cupcakes, chips, hot sauce, dips, and veggie sticks.

Our plan for the day was: board buses to attend high school Christmas program, return to our own school for lunch, have class Christmas party, open class gifts, and finally, go home for two weeks.

The Christmas program was even better than the year before. The high school dance squad moved to "I Saw Mommy Kissing Santa Claus" in really cute elf costumes. All the girls in our class wished they could dance like that. Camila said she wished she was an elf, and one of the boys told her she already had the ears for it. Camila took it as a compliment and giggled.

At lunch, we ate thin slices of pizza. It was just enough. It left plenty of room for the party food. Ms. Hamlin had set up everything by the time we returned to class. We attacked the shelf as if we hadn't eaten anything at all. I sat in the corner with a plate of potato chips, and kept to myself.

Some of the boys dared Roy to drink a bottle of Tabasco sauce while Ms. Hamlin wasn't looking. He chugged half, then ran to the bathroom with the emergency pass hanging from the chalkboard. Would he be okay? Would he have to go to the hospital and get his stomach pumped? And maybe he should go home early. Everyone wondered these things in a nervous whisper. But Roy came back and told Ms. Hamlin he just had a little belly ache. It was nothing. He'd be okay.

An hour before school let out, Ms. Hamlin opened the supply closet, unveiling a pile of presents carefully wrapped in baby blue butcher paper and homemade ribbons. Most classes had gift exchanges for Christmas. Ms. Hamlin, coming from a different place and having different ideas, did things differently. She asked our parents for five dollars each. She posted a list on the bulletin board that included: books, fashion school accessories, posters, and basically anything from the book fair catalog that cost about that much. She then asked us to write letters in essay form telling her about our top three choices and why. I picked all books. One was fun reading, one was for learning, and one was a journal.

Some kids guessed what they were getting by the shape of the butcher paper. I knew mine was a book, but I just didn't know which one.

On the count of three, we tore away the butcher paper. The boys found things like trading cards, wristbands, magnifying glasses, and insect jars. The girls found things like posters of their favorite pop stars, calendars of puppies, charm bracelets, and bead kits.

That is, except for me. Beneath the blue paper

in my hands lay *A Night Alone in the Universe*. I knew it was the book Nora would've picked if she'd had the courage. It was the type of book that made science okay, but still not good enough for a clone.

At home, I showed Apá what I got for a gift. They didn't do gifts at the junior high so the twins had nothing to show. Clark had gotten a box of chocolates and already eaten half.

That night, after I read some of my book, I slept cradled by a universe that was large and mostly empty all around me. It made me feel even smaller and more alone. But maybe that wasn't my world. Maybe what lay beyond those four walls didn't matter.

My family was a solar system. My father was the sun, and the rest of us were planets rotating all around him. This world of mine was small, but it was the only thing that fit or maybe it was the only one I fit in.

Special

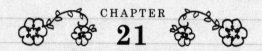

CHAPTER
21

W hat do you want from Santa?" Apá asked. Christmas was a few days away. I wasn't sure what I wanted. I wanted something fun, but I was growing up. I waited for everyone else to say first. Clark asked for a baseball mitt. Angel Jr. asked for a videogame joystick. Sly Silvia whispered hers in Apá's ear.

I told him, "I don't know. What do you want?"

"Love," he said. Love. That was all. That was easy enough. I loved him every minute of every day. No, every second of every minute of every day.

On the night of the twenty-third, Silvia and Apá snuck away to Super Wal-Mart. They came back with a giant turkey and several mysterious bags. They put the turkey in a sink full of ice to thaw and stashed the bags in my parents' bedroom.

That night, Silvia didn't drown me out of her sleep with her headphones. The gravel of her nighttime voice found me and whispered secrets in the dark. "I know what everyone is getting for Christmas," she said. "Amá is getting hoop earrings. Clark is getting a baseball mitt. Angel Jr. is getting a videogame controller. I'm getting a giant stuffed animal to sit on my bed. Everyone is getting exactly what they asked for, but you didn't ask for anything."

I listened for more, but it was quiet. Silvia had drifted asleep or she wanted me to think I wasn't getting anything. I knew Apá would get me something special. I didn't need to tell him anything. I'd love whatever it was. These were the thoughts unraveling inside my head. I got up and walked to my parents' room. I slowly turned the knob, but the door wouldn't budge.

"We're wrapping presents!" Apá hollered from the other side.

The following morning, Amá took advantage of the last few hours of holiday shopping and picked up a present for Apá. She spent the rest of the day at home with us.

After the sun set, Apá turned the space heater

up to its hottest setting. It got colder. He described the fireplace in the new house to Amá as he did so. "You'll see. I ordered some really nice grey marble tiles for the trim. This time next year we're going to be sitting in front of a fire."

We ate dinner late. Clark fell asleep. It was just as well because he was the type to try and wait up for Santa. After dinner, Amá and Apá told stories about their Christmases growing up.

Amá told us how they didn't eat turkey for Christmas dinner like us. They ate spicy pork tamales instead. She and my aunts snuggled in blankets in front of my grandma's cast iron stove late into the night waiting for my abuelita to stir the leftover corn mix into homemade *champurrado*. It was a thick and delicious hot chocolate drink.

"The *champurrado* from Juarez is mud in comparison," she told us. "Warm blankets and *champurrado* was our Christmas. There were no presents. You kids have it good. Our presents didn't come until *El Día de los Reyes Magos*. The Three Kings came two weeks later and brought us socks and oranges. Those little things were luxuries. I waited for them all year long."

"You should make us *champurrado*," Angel Jr. said. We burst into laughter. Our bellies were full, and he was still asking for food.

Apá told us about the warm Christmases in California. "We decorated palm trees," he joked and didn't say much else. He got up and went outside to smoke a cigarette. Amá didn't stop him. She told us that thinking of his sister in California sometimes made him sad because she was his only other family, and she was so far away.

My aunt had been too young to be a mother and too old to be a sister when their parents died, but he had followed her to California anyway. They had become close back then. He only saw her once a year now. It was too expensive and crowded in the truck for us all to visit, so Apá and Angel Jr. traveled on the Conejo Express. The rest of the year, Apá settled for a phone call.

"*Navidad* in California wasn't that much different than here," was all that Apá said when he finally came back inside. Christmases in El Paso weren't exactly warm even though we lived in the desert. Sometimes it snowed and the snow melted before it hit the ground. Sometimes we got enough snow to build a snowman. More times the sun shone, but the air was still cold enough to wear a heavy coat and scarf.

"Can we spend Christmas in California one day?" Silvia asked him.

"One day, *mija*," Apá answered, and I knew he really wanted to by the way he got happy again.

At midnight, Apá began pulling the presents out into the living room, and Amá told us to wake up Clark. We took turns opening presents from youngest to oldest. First we got a bunch of sweaters for school. Next came the good gifts. Clark got his mitt, and then it was my turn. I ripped into the paper to find the most perfect brown teddy bear I'd ever seen.

I hugged my dad and kissed my mom. Silvia's bear was almost like mine, except white and bigger. Angel Jr. got his videogame thing. Amá got her earrings, and Apá got a watch heavy-duty enough to wear when he was building. Amá kissed him on the cheek and told us that our real present would be the new house.

We were all exhausted and went to bed right away. Silvia put her white bear on the shelf so that it wouldn't get dirty. I put my bear next to it, and we both stood there for a minute. I loved mine. "I'm going to name him Murray," I told her. It was the first thing that popped into my head. I'd never named anything before or talked to imaginary friends. It was something only kids on TV and in books did.

"You can't name him that, your bear is Mexican because it's brown," Silvia said, trying to be funny.

I didn't laugh. I didn't pay attention. His name was Murray. I hugged him and climbed into bed.

Murray, Murray was soft and furry, and he was mine.

THE JOB

CHAPTER
22

Old people needed taking care of every day. That meant Amá was on the roster to work during most of our break.

"Those Christmas gifts didn't pay for themselves," she said. We had to stay at home all day by ourselves. No one out; no one in. Angel Jr. and Silvia protested for a minute. They'd made plans to hang out with their friends. In the end, Silvia came up with the idea of going to work with Apá instead. Apá agreed.

Apá had been working on the house for a couple of months and wanted to finish in the spring. He was on a tight schedule. Amá warned us about getting in his hair. No one complained. Working with Apá was the best.

When he began building, Apá no longer had full-time help. He had a lot of material, a lot of experience, and just a little help from Tomás. Tómas dropped in once in a while and helped Apá with the major stuff.

There were a couple of other guys who owed him favors too. Apá had done work for them, and they were paying him back with the same. They'd built houses together before, if only in pieces. They helped him pour down the cement foundation and put up the wall supports. They helped him lay down the water and sewer pipes. They helped him place the bricks and fit the ceiling. That was the shell of our home. Then Apá wired the electricity and phone.

Now he was going to finish the walls, the tiles, and the rest of the house's innards and we'd get to help.

Apá made us honorary workers. He handed me a hammer and a jar full of bent-up nails to straighten. I sat there all morning with my jar. If we did a good job, he'd pay us with potato chip money.

Angel Jr. lent a hand with the tiles on the floors and the shower walls. Silvia picked out paint colors. Clark and I mostly did what we'd done before when we stayed home from school with Apá. We sorted his tools and handed them to him. He never asked for anything sharp or electric. He didn't want us getting hurt.

"How about school? Is school better now?" Apá asked me.

"No," I told him. "I still don't have a lot of friends."

"Well, you don't need many friends, you just need good ones," he told me. I guess my parents didn't have a whole lot of friends either. There were tons of people on the street who always said "hi" to my dad. That made it seem like he knew everybody. But if I really thought about it, the only grown ups who had always been around were my mom's sisters who were kind of like her best friends. And Tomás.

"I just wish I had a best friend, like you and Tomás," I told Apá.

"Well, Tomás is a good friend, but your amá is my best friend," he corrected. Family came first.

"You have us," he added. I thought about Silvia. She wasn't going to be my best friend. I guess my dad was my best friend just like he was Amá's.

For lunch, we chopped up jalapenos, tomatoes, and onions. Apá threw them in a skillet with leftover turkey, and Silvia warmed up flour tortillas. It was mostly white meat. Even my dad dug in. It was okay as long as he didn't eat too many tortillas. We polished off the last of the leftover Christmas food in no time.

After we ate, we sat around and talked like old friends. "If your mother and I separated, who would you go with?" he joked. I smiled. I loved being there with Apá. No answer was necessary. I loved my mom, but my dad never made us eat vegetable stew or got on us for sitting too close to the television. Sometimes, feeling a little guilty for playing favorites, I told him that it didn't matter because he and my mom were going to be together always and forever.

After Apá finished the bathroom tiles, he let me caulk the bathtub. I squeezed stuff that looked like toothpaste onto the corners of the tub so that the water didn't leak out.

"I don't mind the old house," I told him. But Apá wanted something that belonged to us.

The next few days of working with my dad weren't at all what I thought real work would be. It wasn't like doing chores or schoolwork. Helping Apá made me feel important. He joked around and told us stories about adventures on his job. He told us he had found a nest of snakes once. Another time he got to meet the owner of a Whataburger who was a close friend of a client. We were having so much fun that I didn't even tell Silvia or Amá about the dozens of cigarette butts I found in an upturned flower pot at the new house. I didn't want things to get serious.

Those days with Apá made me want to stay home sick for the rest of the school year. I'd do anything and put up with anything to stay with my apá. One day, I sat up against a freshly painted wall wearing one of my favorite outfits. It was a red running suit with white stripes along the sides and later a big paint stain on the leg. I didn't cry about the stain.

I didn't even complain. Staying home from school with Apá was worth it.

I asked Apá if I could help him for the next few months. The teacher could send home my reading with Clark.

"I love having you kids around too, *mija*," Apá said. "I miss you when you're at school, but I can't let you stay home. I didn't have the same opportunities as you kids. You need to make the most of them."

So we made a pact, just him and me. I'd return to school, and Apá would let me help him after school on the days I didn't have GT.

GoOd Ball

CHAPTER
23

Once the second half of the school year got going, I had a routine that didn't include worrying about hateful girls. The school year would end in a few months, and I worked hard at ignoring how the enemy group acted toward me.

When I didn't have GT, I walked the short distance to where my dad was working on our new house. He was working later and longer, sometimes until sundown and sometimes on weekends. I helped him sweep up and put away tools.

If it was still light out when my dad finished for the day, we piled bricks at each end of the construction site and used them as soccer goals. It made me think of summer when our whole family went to the park and played for hours.

Back then, when we got tired, my dad drove away and came back with buckets of delicious greasy chicken for a picnic. Now, we just went just home.

There were other ways playing soccer after-school was different. We played for shorter periods, and mostly one-on-one. Sometimes my brothers or sister joined us. Other times they did things with their friends or stayed home. Apá and I still had fun. He let me win, but made me work hard. That's how my kick got stronger and stronger.

By the time the big school tournament started, I was breathing soccer thanks to my afternoons with Apá. I couldn't think about anything else. I concentrated on those balls zooming by on the dry yellow grass that didn't break when we ran through it—grass that bent and sprung back up. Everything around us stopped in the middle of that soccer field when we played.

The enemy girls probably wanted nothing more than to see me warming the bench. Only, it didn't work that way. Their popularity couldn't keep me from playing.

We didn't pick our soccer teams. The teams were divided by class and grade. Girls only played girls. Boys only played boys. Sixth graders only played sixth graders. All of the classes played against each other. We practiced regularly and played one official game each week. We played again for places according to how many games we won by the end of the season. Each grade got its own championship tournament that way.

To us, winning the tournament was like winning the World Cup. It was the one time when it didn't matter if a kid spoke funny English, got bad grades or had an A-class pedigree. A kid just had to want it bad enough to try really hard. In a tournament like this, a person didn't have to be liked either. She or he could be the most hated kid in the world. And if they were good, everyone started liking them.

The girls on my school team still didn't talk to me much, but some of the girls from the other classes called out things to me when we weren't playing against them, like, "Good shot. Go Chela!" It was Angelica, Bianca, Clarissa, and Yaretzi, the girls from my fifth grade class. My dad said that meant I still had their respect.

I wanted to say that Nora and them were no good at the game. That would've been a lie. Most of the girls on our team were good for some reason or another. Nora used to go to the park with my family. She was smaller than many of us, and faster. She hadn't grown or changed much, except for getting rid of the glasses.

It was also true that Camila and her clones went to soccer camp the summer before. Every time something went right on the field for her, Camila made sure to mention that when she was in soccer camp she did something even more spectacular. Soccer camp happened through the Boys and Girls Club. I hadn't been allowed to go because of the *cholos* and *cholas* that sometimes hung around their building throwing gang signs.

By the end of the tournament, our class was up for first place. We lost only one game. We held the same record as 6-C, the team we would play for the championship. Their girls looked like eighth graders. Some of them actually should've been eighth graders but flunked a couple of grades somewhere along the line.

The day of the big championship game, everyone was nervous. I had to remind myself to breathe. We tried to create chances early on, quickly switching the ball right and left using both wings while trying to find a kink in 6-C's defense. We were weaker, but faster.

Nora, who was a midfielder, hit a shot off the left post and missed. 6-C responded immediately. We were deadlocked. Camila gained control of the ball, but there were too many defenders on her. She needed to pass. She looked up and saw only me. Who knows what she was thinking. Probably that she had no choice. She delivered the ball to me as I shrugged off a 6-C girl and ran close to the goal. I headed the ball into the net.

Zooooom! Goooooooooooooolaso!

One to zero 6-A! We were the new champions!

Everyone was cheering, even Camila and Nora. We jumped and cheered so hard that I sweated more than when we played.

As we got ready to go back to class, it happened. The queen of our grade said something nice to me for the first time ever outside of class. "Good game," she said. I nodded my head and walked back to our classroom.

At lunch, Camila came over to me and said, "So I was thinking that maybe we can be friends. We'll see you after school at GT!"

Then she walked away, just like that.

Normal

CHAPTER
24

Camila invited me to walk with them after GT. Then she invited me to walk home with them every day and hang out. When I told Roy, he said he didn't mind. He was doing better in school and said he'd just ride his bike home.

That evening, I told Apá all about the soccer game and the change of heart in my classmates. I was glad he hadn't let me stay home sick for the rest of the school year. I was glad the girls in my class finally wanted to be my friends, but I'd promised to help him with the house.

"Don't worry about me," Apá said. "The house will be finished soon enough. Then you'll be sorry you gave up the chance to be around kids your own age."

"But I want to be with you too," I told him.

"You can come with me on the weekend," he said.

I thought about the next day until I was too tired to think. I was the most excited about talking to Nora again.

The first thing the girls told me at school the

following morning was the set of rules for being in their group.

"You can't change your look in a big way or wear something we haven't seen, unless we say it's okay," Toña said.

"You can't talk to anyone we don't talk to, and you can't talk to anyone of us more than the others," Camila added.

"You can't like any boys without telling the rest of us," Brenda threw in.

"For example, Brenda likes Aaron," Camila blurted.

"Hey!" Brenda protested. "You can't tell her that. Tell her who YOU like!"

"We'll tell her who everyone likes once she tells us who she likes," Camila said.

"I don't like anyone," I told them. It wasn't a lie.

Camila smiled like a cat. "Well, when you do, we have to be the first ones you tell. Then we'll tell you who we all like. When you're popular, you just have to be careful who you let in," she said, matter-of-factly.

Those were their rules.

Nora didn't say much of anything until later. Since there was no GT, we helped the librarian shelve books after school.

Nora tried to tell me something about the beginning of the school year. "I'm glad we get to talk again," she said. She was very sorry and wanted to explain. But the librarian told us to keep it down. I whispered to Nora that she didn't need to explain. Someone shushed us again.

I was actually glad that the librarian wanted us to zip it. The truth was I just wanted to forget about before. If I stopped to remember, it might all come back: the silence, the mean jokes, the snickering. I wanted to enjoy just being a normal kid again.

The next day Camila gave us little pink heart-shaped pins to wear. Nora said that she did nice things like that every now and again. Camila's talking to me made it okay for other girls in our class to follow. When it was time to study for our spelling test, a couple of girls even asked to partner up with me. I picked Nora, of course. Even then, we only really did things as a group. That was the rule.

Our first week of being friends, Camila called me on the telephone at home and told me we would all wear khakis to school on Friday. I would've worn a paper bag over my head if she had asked. It was the same every Friday. That became our group thing.

"Those girls aren't really your friends," Silvia said to me one afternoon. But hers were the words of someone who'd never had to eat lunch or walk home alone. At night I stared at the ceiling of our bedroom for a long time before I fell asleep. I didn't feel so small.

HOUSE oF Prayers

CHAPTER
25

Apá worked on the house alone and I hung out with Nora, Camila and the others. I didn't help him as much, even though we'd agreed. While I felt guilty about it, I told myself that he'd worked all alone even before me. He'd be fine. He had said so himself.

Besides, I still helped him on the weekends. And when the house he called our dream home was finished—just as Apá predicted—I didn't feel so bad.

After the bare bones of its frame were dressed and all the dangling wires tucked away, it looked like many houses in our neighborhood, only new and bright. All on one floor, there were three bedrooms, two bathrooms, a fireplace, and a driveway paved smooth. My favorite part was the slippery marble that squeaked under the rubber soles of our shoes as we walked.

Maybe it wasn't anything extraordinary, but to me it was absolutely beautiful. Our sweat had gone into it. My dad had built it. We had helped at least a little.

We moved in one weekend, piling everything into my dad's truck. Silvia and I moved all the small stuff from our room ourselves. Apá and Angel Jr. loaded the beds. Apá's friend Tomás and some of the other men he'd worked with helped with the really heavy stuff, like the stove, the refrigerator, and the washing machine. After they finished, they sat outside grilling steaks and telling stories in the dark. Apá wasn't supposed to eat red meat, but it was a special occasion.

Inside, there were toys, books and other things scattered everywhere. The house looked lived in, in a good way. It was like we had always been there. We promised to pick up the following day. Amá didn't seem upset about it.

That night I found her and Apá sitting on the couch. I said goodnight before I went to bed. I listened to Amá thank Apá as I walked away. He whispered to her that he was a man filled with pride to be able to give his family a real home. It was what he'd always wanted. The house was ours, not someone else's, not a bank's. It was ours. He probably fell asleep on my mom's shoulder whispering those things.

Our first morning officially in the house, I pulled out the soccer ball and asked Clark if he wanted to play. "You keep it down, and no soccer inside the house," my mom told us as she passed by on her way to the kitchen. We didn't want her getting mad and taking off her *chancla*. That's why, when she was gone, we started a game of indoor basketball instead.

We had a full game going on inside the newly crowded living room walls. The ball bounced off the three-dimensional glass-encased waterfall, off the plastic grade-school trophies, and off the gold-trimmed encyclopedias. Soon, Silvia, Angel Jr. and Apá joined. Clark maneuvered the orange ball with his stubby fingers. But, no matter how hard I tried, I was the one Gonzalez who couldn't bounce anything other than sound. The ball kept rolling away from me. "Man, you're terrible," Angel Jr. said.

The tightness of a good cry rose up within my chest, but my dad smiled. "*¡Si, se puede!*" he said to me as he passed me the ball again and winked.

"YES, YOU CAN is a soccer phrase. That's the only game she knows how to play!" Angel Jr. interrupted.

"At least I know something!" I shot back.

"YES, YOU CAN applies to everything," Apá said and smiled even bigger.

The corners of his mouth twitched as he fought a different type of steady rumbling, one which threatened to explode into happy thunder. "It's like glue." His contagious laughter finally erupted, and I forgot about feeling sorry for myself. We all laughed until the corners of our eyes started leaking.

Things were good. I didn't let anything ruin my mood. I was having fun, even though basketball wasn't my game. Right then and there, I was the happiest girl who ever lived. I hugged my dad hard. Then I told him so over and over again.

We didn't worry about being loud, even though Amá had warned us. She never stayed mad, especially at Apá. Apá was a strong still oak. We hid under his branches like shadows. Even when he laughed a thunderous laugh, those branches shook only ever so slightly.

That's how I thought it would always be—before a second stroke of bad luck came to uproot him.

CHAPTER
26

Amá woke us up for school the next morning, and told us to keep it down because Apá was still in bed. We fumbled around trying to figure out where we'd put things after the move. Never mind that it was late for Apá to be sleeping. He was the one who usually woke the rest of us up. He never complained, but he was probably relieved to get a chance to sleep in.

I snuck into his room and kissed Apá good-bye before leaving for school. He smiled as he slept, and I wondered if he dreamed of something nice. I got the urge to make the sign of the cross on him. My mom always told us to cross ourselves when we went to sleep. I did this as quietly as possible so that I didn't wake him.

When I got back home from school, my abuelita and her luggage were the only ones around. My grandma had been staying in Juarez with one of my aunts, but my mom hadn't said anything about her coming to our house.

I kissed her on the cheek. I asked her if she liked the new house, and if she knew where my dad had gone. She was hesitant and answered yes to the house. Then she asked me to sit down. She told me Apá wasn't home because he was at the hospital. Amá was by his side.

Apá'd had another stroke. A stroke—I repeated the words inside my head. It was a slap across the face that hurt so bad because I hadn't seen it coming.

We wanted to visit my dad, but Abuelita said that the doctors at the hospital wouldn't let us in. It was just like before. Only kids older than fifteen were allowed. She gave me that same excuse about some bug going around, and the hospital not wanting kids around the patients.

I wanted to at least wait in the hospital lobby. She wouldn't let us. She wouldn't let us do anything. So when she wanted us to say a rosary with her, I refused. She didn't make Angel Jr. and Silvia do those things. I stomped into our room where Silvia listened to music on her headphones, still unpacking stuff. I locked the door. She just rolled her eyes, turned her back to me and ignored me.

"*Niña malcriada*. God is going to castigate you!" Abuelita yelled at me from the living room and went off to light half-a-dozen candles with Clark's help. I heard the muffled sounds of their prayers hit the wall and trickle down to the floor. I went to sleep without even doing the sign of the cross on myself.

Apá had faced the darkness before, and this time didn't feel the same. Amá didn't make us stay home from school. She said Apá was talking and everything. Angel Jr. even snuck in to see him. Everyone made it sound like Apá was fine.

The school week went by, and I went about my days like usual.

I even stayed shelving books at the school library with Nora and them on the Friday before our spring break began. I got home at four-thirty. I took ice cream from the refrigerator when no one was looking. I ate it in the bathroom. I ate it fast so it wouldn't melt and drip onto the new floors to give away my secret.

When my *tía* Tere's Impala drove up broadcasting Amá's return with its whiny wheels, I ran out to meet them. One by one, my mom and my aunts stepped out of the car with their heads down low. I was surprised to see them, especially so early. No one said anything. Then I saw what I hadn't before. I felt it. Maybe it was my punishment, like Abuelita had said.

There were tears streaming down my aunts' cheeks. Amá's own cheeks were stained with tears. Angel Jr. locked himself in his room. One of our aunts took Silvia aside, while Amá held my little brother and said, "Your father got in his pickup and drove it to heaven."

My heart held itself like a breath caught inside my throat. I ran into the bathroom.

"No, no, NO! Apá was supposed to get better." I screamed a hollow terrible noise, like an animal. I don't know when I breathed again. I don't know when I left the bathroom. I just know I did.

CHAPTER
27

I ground my teeth and wondered how something could go so terribly wrong. If Apá had taken real medicine, if he had stopped smoking or stayed on his diet, if we had prayed...maybe this would all be different.

I crossed myself and clasped my hands together tightly. "God forgive me. God FORGIVE me. God forgive ME. God give me. God give me this one thing I ask of you—give me back my apá..."

I heard voices praying in the living room too. It was a thick sad sound, like waiting for molasses. I didn't like molasses, and I didn't like that sound.

It was too late. I grabbed my bear from the dresser, lay in my bed and cried until there was no water left in me, only the taste of salt on my face. I thought that no one knew or could know. No one knew unless they knew pain. No knew what it was like not to want to open their eyes again.

I closed my eyes, but I didn't sleep that night. No one did. We prayed for what must've been days, until Angel Jr. came in the room and said it was time to get up and go to the funeral home.

It was spring break, almost Easter, and I wanted to get ready for that instead. I wanted to sit in the kitchen filling eggshells with confetti to dip in vinegar dye. That would've meant none of this was happening.

But Amá's face gave it away. Amá looked a hundred years old. I guess it fit, since Apá once joked that he was a hundred and fifty-three.

At the funeral home, everyone sat by the coffin and prayed even more. They went up and looked at Apá. Everyone told me I should go up to the coffin and pay my last respects. I don't know why, but I didn't want to see him lying there dead. Everyone said I had to. They said it to my brother Clark too. They told him he was a man now, so he had to. He did. But I couldn't.

Amá said there were people who only turned up when someone died, that death made us come together. There were people there like my aunts and Tomás. There were others like my dad's sister who came and went, and still others I'd never seen in my life. I wanted them to go away. I wanted Apá to come back.

The day of the funeral, my mom pulled on a black dress and pantyhose. Then she laid out church clothes for all of us. I had to wear one of Silvia's dresses because the ones hanging on my side of the closet didn't fit anymore. Amá grabbed her rosary, stood by the front window looking out, and waited for us to dress.

When I was ready, I walked into the living room.

"Your father didn't want you to cry. Remember what he used to say. Men don't cry. You're a man now. You have to remember," Amá repeated to Clark as she buttoned his best Sunday shirt.

I closed my eyes, and I could hear Apá's voice say almost the same thing. *Cuando me muera no quiero que me lloren, pues por algo pasan las cosas.*

He didn't want us to cry when he died; things happened for a reason.

But there could be no reason for something that was this terrible.

My mom handed me a bunch of yellow daisies tied together with a string. I counted eleven, one for every year of my life even if I felt older.

"Put these on the coffin when they begin with the soil," she told me. Never mind that that wasn't what Apá wanted. He told us when his sickness began. *Quiero que me quemen y tiren mis cenizas 'pa'l río. Quiero que me dejen allá de donde vine. Yo vine v cerros floridos.* He wanted to be burned, to be thrown into the river, to return to where he came from. He came from the florid hills.

We squeezed into my aunt's Impala, and she drove us to the church. It was stuffy inside, and the dirt in the air clung to my face. Miss Mickey, the old woman who lit the candles and cleaned up after mass, was extra nice. She smiled at us. I hoped that she knew something I didn't know because I sure couldn't smile.

Sunday mass always lasted forever. I thought it would be like that, but it wasn't. Everything happened fast, like a nightmare with things flashing by. The priest did his thing. My brother and *tíos* carried the coffin out. We followed them down the church aisle to the car that was driving us to the cemetery. I bowed my head, but still felt people's eyes on me as we walked by. I wanted Miss Mickey to pinch me so I would wake up.

But it wasn't a bad dream. It was worse.

We made our way to Everest Cemetery in the funeral home's car. The driver called it The Limousine. But it wasn't really a limo, except maybe in a horror movie. Two policemen on motorcycles rode ahead of us. They did this for all funerals.

Sometimes, in the soccer field at school or the park outside, we saw the policemen and the limousine and all the cars following down the Border

Highway. We would stand still and be quiet for a minute. Maybe there was a group of kids someplace doing the same for Apá.

At the cemetery they opened the coffin again so that people could say good-bye forever. They told us Apá was watching. He loved us. He was an angel. My father's name was Angel too. I guess Diosito must've planned it that way. But I still couldn't go up there. I stood back.

My mother was leaning over the coffin with tears running down her face. A woman went up to the coffin, looked in, and shrieked. Then everyone wanted to see what happened. There were flowers everywhere, mostly stamped onto the heels of their dress shoes. Someone fainted. That someone was my abuelita. My *tías* sprinkled cold holy water in her face to wake her up.

The women said a miracle happened: that my apá was crying. Everyone pushed forward. Someone pulled me over to where it smelled bad of old lady perfume.

The smell was worse than Sundays.

Sundays were sad, but they went just as sure as they came.

Death was a whole other thing.

I didn't mean to look, but everyone pushed. Rosary in one hand and hat in the other, there was a single tear on his brown rubbery cheek. It slowly slid down to the side of his nose until it disappeared. I quickly looked away and put my hands to my face.

Those tears were not real. That was not my father. I tried to erase the dead picture from my mind. That was not him. That was not my apá.

They prayed again, talked and put the coffin in the ground. Amá reminded me to put the daisies on the casket. I threw them in and quickly walked away because as far as I could tell that wasn't Apá. Apá told us not to cry and he wasn't crying either.

I closed my eyes real tight, and saw him exactly as he was. Apá had soft skin, and he was alive.

After the Wake

CHAPTER
28

Amá said we had to mourn and didn't let us turn on the television. I looked up the word mourn in the dictionary. It meant to feel or show sorrow. I knew we'd be doing that whether the television was on or not. A feeling couldn't be turned off by a power switch like an electrical appliance.

We were still off from school for spring break, and there was nothing we could do other than feel very sad to know that no matter how long we waited, Apá wasn't coming home. I waited for him by a tree anyway, pretending to squish berries into the dirt until the sun went down, and Silvia came to tell me, "Come inside, stupid."

Amá sent away my abuelita and my aunts, telling them she'd manage. Everyone went home with Tupperwares full of leftovers from the funeral reception. Amá had asked for time off from work so she stayed home with us.

In the coming days, I watched the people around me: Amá, Silvia, and my brothers. It made me even sadder to look at them.

Amá got up each morning and pulled on a black running suit. She fed us and did the things that needed to get done. When the sweeping was finished and the dishes were dry, she walked around like a zombie obsessed with finding more things to clean or put away.

Sometimes I caught her staring into the closet. She didn't move any of Apá's clothes. It was like she was trying to figure something out. She didn't talk much. Her lips were small and tight. Once in a while I saw them fighting a twitch. Maybe she was trying not to break down thinking of Apá. I wasn't supposed to see that, but I saw all kinds of things.

While Amá wanted to swallow the sting, Silvia wanted to holler at the world. She was fourteen, going on eighteen. She feathered her hair at night, and slept very still like a mummy in a coffin. She sprayed it stiff again in the morning. She wasn't allowed to wear lipstick, but she secretly stained her lips the color of pomegranates with a tube stolen from my *tia's* purse. She did it in the bathroom and hid the lipstick in her shoe.

Her friends all had boyfriends who they promised to hang out with at the park during break. They called her on the phone. They begged her to hang out too. They said that if she didn't, that boy Jimmy, from the Dairy Queen and later the swimming pool, would forget her. She told them that she couldn't, to keep an eye out, something horrible had happened at home. Then she sobbed loudly into the receiver. We weren't supposed to use the phone, but she did. She put on her secret lipstick, and cried that all she wanted was a life like everyone else's.

Angel Jr. acted like he just wanted to forget. He was the only one of us kids to visit Apá at the hospital. Angel Jr. was tall, taller than Apá and bragged that he could even pass for sixteen. He'd snuck in that way. No one knew what Apá had told him, but Angel Jr. hung onto those words anyway.

And, just like they told Clark, they told Angel

Jr. not to cry. He hadn't. Maybe inside or at night he had. He lived inside himself, with no interest in the outside. Soon enough, the disinterest turned to anger. He raged that he was enlisting in the army as soon as he turned eighteen. The army recruiters had a table at the grocery store. They hung around like starving dogs.

"You'll become a citizen sooner that way. Then you'll really be able to make all your dreams come true. You'll be practically American."

But Angel Jr. was already American, born in Texas, and only fourteen. He just wanted to be far away where Apá's absence might fade.

Clark, on the other hand, cried and cried and cried. He didn't play with his toys. He stuffed his matchbox cars in a plastic bag and buried them underneath Apá's truck. He cried in the bathroom. He cried holding a ball. He cried putting peanut butter on a piece of toast. He cried trying to tie his shoelaces. He cried when someone looked at him straight in the face. He cried because no matter what Amá said, he was still only seven and not even a little man. He cried because they told him not to cry.

None of us were the same. None of us would ever be the same. Being at home was like being in trouble and waiting for Amá to come after us with her *chancla*. Except: there was no way out of it.

And, on top of anger and fear, there was a terrible sadness. I wanted Silvia to talk to me like she did to her friends because only she could know how it felt. I would've even settled for one of my brothers, but we didn't talk. We'd stopped talking long before. There was no real reason—just that our ages had made us different.

I thought about what we'd be doing with Apá. "Maybe we could color eggs," I told Amá. Then I heard Clark cry again. Amá went to him and hugged him.

"Is there going to be an Easter?" he asked.

"We'll have a nice quiet dinner," Amá told him. He was the reason that she finally changed her mind about the television.

She told us a story. Before I had any brothers or a sister, before I was even a shadow, my amá was a little girl in a little town where everyone prayed. She was my age the first time she heard that great American invention: the radio. When her uncle moved to the United States and sent one home as a present, the whole town tuned in. They listened for three weeks straight.

When the town deacon died, they left the house only long enough for the wake. In those times, it was a custom to mourn for at least two months without any diversions. Of course, in those days the radio was a whole other thing. The town prayed and put on their black shawls, but the radio stayed, with its peacock feathers of sound, high up on its perch.

Amá told us she was shrouded in silence, but she was going to turn on the television for us. She turned it on with the volume extra loud. She put on Saturday morning cartoons. She looked at me looking at her.

"You can't grow up yet," she said, as if it hadn't been happening for some time.

She lay down on her bed with the bedroom door open. She held Apá's picture and whispered something only for him. She didn't cry in front of us. She didn't talk to us about Apá. She didn't give into her heartache. Her silence was truly a desperate song of love.

FRIENDS and MONSTERS

CHAPTER
29

I don't know why it happened the way it did. The first person I saw when I got back to school was Camila. It wasn't Nora who'd been my best friend and who I'd known most of my life. It was Camila.

Camila stood in front of me wearing squeaky new sneakers with spotless shoelaces. Her bright pink and green outfit was new. She had a different haircut that was much shorter. She was practically doing jumping jacks, looking like she was about to split open like a ripe watermelon. There were no A-girls behind her. I was the first person she saw too.

"I had the best vacation. I went to the beach in Corpus Christi. I got a new bathing suit. We rented a van, and my whole family went. See how I have some sun on my nose. Look. I get freckles. I brought back sand. It's in a jar in my backpack. I'll show you when everyone else gets here," Camila blurted excitedly.

She was sure that no one could top that. "What'd you do?"

"I went to my dad's funeral," I muttered with a

stiff tongue before I thought better of it. Maybe I only imagined I muttered. Maybe she didn't hear me. Maybe my tongue was too dry to have said anything. Maybe she didn't know what to answer. Maybe she didn't do it on purpose, but Camila didn't say anything. Her eyes didn't say anything, and her mouth didn't even twitch.

I felt like my dad didn't exist. I didn't exist. I kept my mouth shut after that. I just listened.

All the kids around us talked about their spring breaks and what they did for Easter. They talked about the new Sunday clothes their parents bought them. The girls were excited about their new dresses. The boys hated having been made to wear slacks and ties. Some kids whispered about cookouts with their family. Other kids bragged about long car trips to visit faraway relatives. Everyone passed around their leftover Easter candy. I took some and put it in my backpack.

Eventually Camila took over again.

"I love the beach," she said. "Your family should go there sometime," she said.

She continued nonstop about her trip and her new clothes. She got three new outfits even though there was only one Easter. Her sisters also bought her new sneakers. She talked and talked without asking any more questions.

Every time another girl in the group arrived, Camila started her story from the beginning and repeated every detail down to the last shoelace. She told the girls how everyone at the beach was wearing short hair, and so she had cut hers. She talked and talked until the bell rang.

Toña and Brenda showed us their new outfits as we walked to class. They both had on skirts from the teen store at the mall. When Toña asked if I got a new outfit too, I squirmed in my clothes, a little embarrassed. I knew that everyone would dress up so I'd dressed up in a nice pair of capri pants and a pattern shirt that I'd worn to church before. We hadn't gotten new outfits, but at least my mom hadn't made us wear black to school.

I wasn't sure what to say, then Nora saved me. She chimed in with a story about how she saw a bunch of junior-high kids making out at the park during break. She'd been on her way downtown with her sister. That's all they talked about until the second bell rang and class started.

I didn't pay enough attention to know if class was the same as usual. I didn't raise my hand when the teacher asked questions. I opened my book to whatever page it landed on. I tried to be as invisible as when I didn't have friends. I snuck tiny marshmallow Easter eggs from my backpack, peeled their plastic wrappers, and popped them into my mouth.

When the teacher called my name for lunch, I got in line out of reflex. I was near the front. I loaded my tray with a sloppy joe and tater tots. I found a table. I sat down. The other girls were still piling things on their trays. I opened my milk carton and took a swig. I felt a little like I might throw up right then and there.

Roy found me and sat with me. He looked at me,

quietly at first. He asked me to put my hand out. I did, and he put out his and dropped a pink Hershey's Kiss onto my palm. For a few seconds he held his hand on top of mine. When I turned my head, Camila was walking towards us, but something was wrong. The blood rose to her face until she was fire red. Then she pivoted, like she was faking in the soccer field, and walked straight in the opposite direction.

Brenda and Toña followed. Camila sat two tables away and called to Nora, who stood in the middle of the cafeteria. She and I looked at each other, trying to figure out why we hadn't all just sat together.

"I thought there was nothing going on with Roy. She's still such a loser. This is why we can't be friends with her," Camila hissed loudly.

I didn't understand. Roy had come to me. She was jealous! That was the big secret of who she liked. That was why she'd hated me so much. But Roy was just my friend.

Before I could explain or think much of the worst,

Nora did something I didn't expect. She shot back at Camila, "Stop being so bossy. You're wrong. Even if you can't be friends with her, I can."

She walked to my table. Nora put down her tray and hugged me. I looked over, and Camila's face was a double angry blister. Roy was already eating his food. Roy was clueless. He probably hadn't even heard that Camila put a *tacha-tacha* on him—put an X on him and called dibs.

I gave Roy my tater tots. He and Nora sat with me until the bell rang. I didn't know what to make of it. I thought I should feel bad, but there was no more room for it. Maybe having real friends was one hundred times better than being Camila's clone. I didn't tell them about Apá. I didn't have to because the look on Nora and Roy's faces told me they knew. Their amás had probably talked to mine. Nora and Roy didn't say anything, and I didn't say anything. I was more like Amá than I thought, and I was glad for the silence.

FRIENDS

The Other Reconciliation

CHAPTER
30

Nora followed me through the maze of kids leaving the building when the bell rang. We made it outside the school fence, and walked home just the two of us for a change.

"Thanks for sticking up for me," I told her.

"You're welcome, but I'm no saint. I was also sticking up for myself. Those girls were never that nice to me. They aren't even that nice to each other. Listen, there's something I want to tell you. I tried to tell you one time at the library. You said I didn't need to, but I do."

"Are you going to tell me that you can't be my friend again?" I asked. She looked at me like I'd hit her in the face with a ball.

"Don't be mad. I guess I deserve that," she said. "I wanted to be popular, and I was. But being part of that group was miserable. Sure, it was nice at first. They talk and talk about clothes and boys. But, that's all they talk about. It gets boring after a while. I thought about trying to make up with you a whole bunch of times. I was scared you'd tell me to bug off, and then I'd end up all alone. I would have deserved that too, huh?"

"I was all alone."

"I am so sorry that I wasn't there for you before. I want us to be best friends again. Can we restart the year, and be best friends again?"

"We can't start the year over, but I can be friends," I said. She hugged me, and I hugged back. Then we both cried. We cried for my dad. We cried for all the things we'd lost. We cried and cried until we started laughing too. We hushed up when we got to my house. She told me she understood that my family wanted to be alone just then, but that she wouldn't be able to sleep just thinking about how we were going to be best friends again.

Nora and I spent all our free time together after that. Camila went back to saying mean things about me when I was alone, but I wasn't alone much. Sometimes Roy even joined us for lunch.

Nora and I walked home together on the days I didn't have GT. I told her all the things I'd never said in front of the clones. We caught up on the whole year that way. I told her about my dad getting sick, about reading alone at the library, about finally getting to use the stuff underneath the bathroom sink, about our new house and about doing homework with Roy.

"I think Roy likes you in that way that makes Camila want to spit," Nora told me. It was because of the way he gave me that Hershey's Kiss.

"No way," I said. "He's my friend. It's not like he squeezed my hand or anything."

She made me admit he was cute, and that it wouldn't be so horrible if she were right. Nora said Roy had always been Camila's secret crush. The Queen believed the most popular boy and girl should be together. She had even carved Roy's name inside a kiss on the big oak tree outside the library in fifth grade.

Nora told me about her sister marrying her boyfriend and moving out. She told me about winning sweepstakes at the science fair, and about life with Camila. She told me how Camila made her feel like they'd always be better than her, even if she were part of their group. She hadn't known them since first grade, and she didn't get into GT. She was always the last one told things or invited places. Nora spilled it all.

She told me how Ms. Hamlin caught Camila cheating off of Brenda. Camila had cried and told Ms. Hamlin that she only did it because she was afraid her own work wasn't good enough since her whole family was made up of smart teachers. Ms. Hamlin felt sorry for her and didn't even tell the principal.

That's when Nora knew for sure that Camila was a big old fraud. "I knew that being let in by that big fake wasn't worth losing my best friend. I just didn't know how to come back," she told me.

"I'm sick of Camila," I told her.

We made a pact not to talk about those girls anymore. We promised to do things because we wanted to and not just to try to measure up to Camila.

My amá let me start going over to Nora's house for an hour or so when I didn't have GT. She also let me invite Nora and Roy over. She said it was only for homework. Nora and I challenged each other to see who could finish their homework first and get the best grades.

One day Ms. Hamlin announced a very important test. It was so her bosses could make sure the kids in our school were doing okay. It would also decide if we were ready to move on to the next grade. It didn't really measure how much we learned in class. It didn't ask questions about the lessons. It was general math, reading, and writing. Every student in the state had to take it.

Nora and I raced to see who'd finish first. I won.

At the end of April, Amá reminded me that I wouldn't be able to study with my friends after school during May because of "Mary Service." She'd only let me miss for GT.

I told Roy and Nora. Roy didn't mind. Nora asked to attend "Mary Service" with me. She'd never done "Mary Service" before. Her parents never made their kids go to church on account of the fact that they could never decide whose church they'd go to. Her dad was Methodist. Her mom was Catholic. Nora didn't really know what either religion was. "I guess that makes me a Cathodist," she said one day.

Silvia rolled her eyes at me when I walked into our room that night and told her Nora would be tagging along for "Mary Service."

"Great," she said, "now there will be two of you."

I couldn't wait.

We walked straight to the church after school. My parents had given me a veil as a present after our final offering the year before. I carried it in my backpack all day. The crown had tiny plastic pearls and plastic leaves that came alive with the sunlight.

I'd been so happy when I got it. Only the girls with crisp white socks and a new dress every week had their own veils.

"It's only for church. It's bad luck to wear it inside the house," Amá had warned. I remembered Amá telling me that same thing when I opened an umbrella inside the house once. I hadn't listened to her then. Like a book, I'd read the umbrella's parts, slid my hands over the smooth handle and each separating bone. But I listened now. I was as scared of what she said as I was of Abuelita's declarations that God would punish me. We'd had enough bad luck and punishment.

Neither Silvia or Nora had their own veils. They sorted through the loan box when we got to the church. It was full of rosaries, hair pins, veils, and other odds and ends.

I spotted Miss Mickey. I walked over to her. "Miss Mickey," I whispered. "Miss Mickey, does God punish people who don't pray?"

"*Mija*, God wants us to pray. He wants to hear from us what is in our hearts. But God doesn't punish." She squeezed my shoulder. It wasn't at all like a pinch. "Have faith, *mija*," she said.

I saw Silvia and Nora walk toward me. I knelt down in one of the pews. I made the sign of the cross on myself and prayed. I concentrated really hard. I prayed for my family. One by one, all the girls knelt down. Miss Mickey passed out the flowers. I counted the flower petals and listened to the nuns' song.

I could've listened to that song forever.

Oh Brothers AND Sister

CHAPTER
31

Amá signed up for a class at the YWCA from six to nine at night. She was studying for a driver's license. She rode the bus to her classes. She might not have been born in a car, but my dad had left a truck, and she was determined to drive it.

Angel Jr. wanted to learn how to drive too. He wasn't old enough for a permit, but he said he wanted to take the red pickup and just drive and forget. He forgot alright. He forgot all about the truck as soon as Amá got him a skateboard. His friends were all into skateboards. They built a ramp in our backyard with Apá's scrap wood. They taught themselves tricks. Their boards slapped across the pavement while I did homework, and on occasion one or another walked by nursing a big scrape.

Amá asked Silvia to babysit Clark and me three nights a week. I objected to having someone watch me. Silvia didn't object to any of it. There was nothing else for her to do since her friends had gotten in trouble for ditching school so they could keep on hanging out at the park. A park worker had busted them and called their parents.

Most of Silvia's friends were grounded until the end of the school year. That meant they weren't even allowed to look at boys. Silvia wasn't with them that day, but she claimed to be sick of boys anyway. That creep from the Dairy Queen, and later the swimming pool, had started talking to some other girl.

My mom told Silvia that she was lucky she hadn't been out there in the park, and that she'd better not be talking to boys until she turned fifteen. Silvia just nodded her head because she'd be fifteen and in high school soon enough.

The first time Silvia was in charge of us, she acted too old for herself. She called us childish, as if she thought she was older than all of us put together. The ancient one probably didn't even remember being eleven anymore and flying across the pavement because she had opened the door to get out of the truck before it stopped moving.

Silvia took us to "Mary Service" first thing after school. Clark went with us too. When we got home, she put on her headphones and ignored us.

She was annoyed that Angel Jr. didn't have to do anything. He didn't even have to watch Clark when we went to church. Angel Jr. just locked himself away with his video games or skateboard. No friends were allowed over when Amá wasn't home. Silvia was taking it out on us.

I told Clark that we had to stick together or we wouldn't stand a chance against Silvia.

Silvia didn't feed us so Clark and I took a can of chicken noodle soup from the cupboard. We opened it and poured it into a plastic container that we stuck in the microwave. Clark set out two bowls before it beeped. I poured half the soup into each one. I sliced a big lime in half, and squeezed it onto our soup. We sat down and ate together. Finally, we rescued all his favorite cars from underneath Apá's truck.

There were two important things that I

remembered about the day Clark was born. The first was that Angel Jr. wanted to name him Superman and Apá suggested Clark instead. Boys!

The second was that Silvia told me Clark was the new baby and I'd no longer be able to sleep in Amá and Apá's bed. As if to prove her right, Clark breast fed even after he could walk. It made me hate him for a long time, but I didn't anymore.

The second time Silvia stayed with us, she did nothing but boss us around. I tried to stay out of her way. Clark and I sat outside where even the *nopales* wanted to shrivel up with thirst. I looked at our backyard with the cactus, dirt, and rocks. I watched a lizard dressed in sand scurry up the side of our house where the grass had grown tall and green. The lizard spy found a place on the porch. The sun sat just right to give enough shade for the lizard's dwarf body. I asked Clark if he wanted a mayonnaise jar to catch it. Clark said no. He liked it and didn't want to scare it away. When Silvia told us we had to come inside and do our homework, I wished she'd just go back to ignoring us.

Clark just took it. He was a nervous little puppy around her. She must have felt bad because she offered to help him with his vocabulary. She held up his red flash cards and made him use the words in sentences.

The first word she held up was mope. "My mom mopes the house when the floor is dirty," he told her.

"That's MOP, silly. Amá 'mops' when she cleans. You 'mope' around the house when you don't get what you want," she corrected him.

He turned the color of the flashcard and giggled. Then she laughed too. By the end of the evening, she even looked like she was having fun. He gave her a hug. She hugged him back.

The third time that Silvia stayed with us, she cleaned out her closet. She piled clothes that she didn't feel like wearing anymore onto my bed. Some of it didn't fit her. Some of it she was just bored with.

I asked her what she was doing with it. She said I could have the clothes if I wanted them. I started hanging them on my side of the closet. It was some of my favorite stuff. I got a couple of new dresses, skirts, shirts, and a hair bandana. They weren't new, but they were new to me. I didn't think she wanted me to hug her, so I gave her a dumb smile. I asked her if she wanted to have some noodle soup with Clark and me. She answered okay, but she turned on the burner and cooked it on the stove top.

We sat on the couch watching a television rerun together. Then Angel Jr. came out of his room and plopped himself down next to us.

"Psst," he said like he was a secret agent, "I got some information."

"What?" Silvia asked. Angel Jr. swore us to secrecy. While he'd been pulling out weeds on the side of the house, Angel Jr. had found an extra cable cord hanging from the neighbor's outside wall. He'd snuck it under the fence.

Silvia asked him if that was illegal. He said he'd pay for it by pulling out the neighbor's weeds. Angel Jr. walked outside. He pushed the cable in from the window, walked back in, and plugged it into the back of the television. He turned it on. It worked!

We watched TV. We laughed and kidded around without getting caught by Amá. In the middle of it all, Clark and I offered to microwave a bag of popcorn. Silvia followed us into the kitchen. She told us to make some of the kind without salt.

I didn't cry for Apá that night.

ANOTHER YEAR

CHAPTER
32

W e finished the project schedule for the after-school program. I was glad I wouldn't have to be alone around Camila anymore, even though I was going to miss the assignments. Ms. Hamlin ordered us pizza and took group pictures. She gave us special GT shirts as good-bye gifts—never mind that she was our daytime teacher and would still see us until school ended. The GT shirts were blue and white with our names embroidered on them.

Ms. Hamlin asked our moms to come at four for refreshments and cookies. The other mothers were dressed up in flowered skirts and buttoned blouses. My mom walked in wearing the blue jeans she always wore to work. To me she looked nicer than any of the dressed-up moms.

Ms. Hamlin gave them a rundown of the program. She even practiced the few Spanish phrases that she'd learned on my amá. Amá smiled politely and shook her head, agreeing with the things Ms. Hamlin said. Ms. Hamlin told her I was one of her most enthusiastic students. I raised my hand more than anyone else.

After we said goodbye, Amá and I walked to the grocery store. "I thought you could help me shop for your birthday dinner," she said.

"What do you want me to cook for you?" It was almost that time, but I hadn't even been counting the days.

"I want homemade flour tortillas with *chiles rellenos*," I told her.

"How many do you want?" she asked me.

"Make fifty. I'm going to eat ten of them!" I told her. We both laughed. Then she called me a little pig. My mouth watered when I thought about the stuffed peppers. She didn't cook for us much anymore. We fed ourselves after school because of her job. I asked for permission to invite Nora to my birthday dinner. The answer was yes.

On the morning I turned twelve, my mom played a Pedro Infante record of *Las Mañanitas* for me to wake up to. It was the official birthday morning song. I didn't tell anyone at school that it was my birthday. I didn't even tell Roy. Ms. Hamlin didn't notice either. That was just how she was. I swore Nora, the only person who knew, to secrecy.

Nora gave me a friendship bracelet with my name on it. She showed me a matching one with her name on it.

"It's to show everyone that we're best friends forever," she said.

That afternoon, they announced the results of our state exams over the school intercom. Everybody did well, but they wanted to let us know there was a kid in our school who actually got the highest score in our grade for the district. Everybody waited for them to say it was Camila. Then the principal read my name over the loud speaker. I'd scored in the ninety-eighth percentile in math and the ninety-ninth percentile in reading and writing.

"We have two reasons to eat cake now," my mom said when I got home and told her.

Nora and I roasted and peeled the peppers for the chiles rellenos. Amá whipped eggs whites until she turned the bowl upside down and nothing fell out. She stuffed the peppers with cheese, dipped them in the egg batter and fried them. Clark helped Silvia frost the cake. Angel Jr. waited outside on his skateboard. When everything was ready, we took the tray of chiles to the dining table where we ate and ate and ate. Nora told my mom how delicious everything was.

After I had about three chiles, Silvia brought out a cake with twelve candles on top. Angel Jr. lit them. They sang me the *Sapo Verde* song just like my dad would've.

Sapo Verde to you, Sapo Verde to you. Sapo Verde, dear Chela...

A *sapo verde* was a green toad, and it rhymed with Happy Birthday. It was a special song even if it was made for teasing because Apá'd always sung it just for us.

"Hurry up and make a wish before the candles melt," I heard Clark say. I made a wish, but I didn't tell anyone what it was, or else it wouldn't come true. I blew hard on the candles. I had to put them all out for the same reason.

"Yay! You got them all," Clark chirped.

My mom brought out a box wrapped in purple tissue paper. It was from everyone, she said. Clark hurried me to open it. He even tore at the paper.

"Hold your pants!" I told him.

It was a brand new pair of sneakers. They were white leather—just like all the girls at school were wearing. I took off my red leather ones that were worn down to the gray at the tips from playing soccer. I put on the new ones. They were the best. I walked around the backyard hugging everyone. Right when I got to Angel Jr., he hugged back and told me he hoped I'd stop being a nerd now that I was older.

I changed back to my old shoes to walk Nora home. When I got back, everyone was sitting around the backyard by my dad's bench. It was hot as summer outside, but I didn't complain.

Amá began with a story about how she was on the girls' basketball team as a kid. They'd even made it to the big city to play in the championship games.

"Amá," Angel Jr. teased, "they didn't play basketball on the *ranchito*—you can't dribble rocks!"

"Oh yeah? Just bring me a ball," she said. Clark ran out and got her the basketball. He passed it to her, and she spun it on the tip of her finger.

"Fancy!" Clark yelled.

"Showoff," said Silvia.

"*Uy*, Amá knows how to have fun," I said.

"That's nothing!" Amá said. She dribbled the ball and passed. I stumbled as I ran to catch it, squealing with excitement. We giggled and screamed.

That night I tossed and turned. I dreamt about my dad. My mom rolled him in on a blue wheelchair that had "Property of County Hospital" stamped on the back in white letters. He wore a brand new shirt and asked if we liked it. I said yes, but then started crying because I remembered ugly things. I told him about it. He replied that the ugly things had never happened.

My dad smiled big. He said it was all a nightmare or maybe a joke. It wasn't a funny joke at all, but I hugged him. We were happy. We did the things we always did. We went to the park and played soccer. We ate leftover cake and watched a movie late at night. He forgot his glasses, and I read the subtitles for him. Then he told me someone should give me a reading trophy. This dream rolled in my head like a movie that kept getting rewound and played over and over again. When I woke up, I felt like taking a small hammer to my head and banging on it because the dream was gone.

All-School girl

CHAPTER
33

Ms. Hamlin pulled me aside in class to tell me that because my test scores were the highest and because I'd made the honor roll all year, I was getting the Outstanding Student in Reading Arts Award for our grade. Nora was getting the Science Award. Camila was getting the Math Award.

Amá was very excited when I told her. She even offered to buy me a new outfit for the awards assembly. It couldn't be something wild. It'd be the last new outfit I'd get for a while. I'd have to wear it for church and other special days too. I was grateful, but I didn't need one. It wouldn't have been fair anyway. We couldn't afford new clothes for all of us, and it was also the last day of school for my sister and brothers.

I decided to wear something from the pile of clothes I got from Silvia when she cleaned her side of the closet. Silvia took good care of her stuff and most of it was practically new. I pulled on a khaki skirt, a purple-button shirt, and my new sneakers.

Everyone in my house dressed up.

"You'd look better with your hair out of your eyes. Can I brush it?" Silvia asked.

I sat on the floor in front of the red couch and let her do whatever she wanted. She pulled my hair up into a ponytail. Angel Jr. and Clark rolled their eyes at us. They had a big hoot and called us "girls." I didn't care; we WERE girls.

The whole sixth grade class knew who was getting most of the awards, but we didn't know who'd win the coveted All-School Girl Trophy. It was the really exciting part of it all. Nora and I felt like we might be close competition for Camila. Each of us was getting at least one other important award. Only the smartest and most popular girl and boy in school ever won, though. We were smart, but Camila was the most popular.

They rang the bell for us to file into the cafeteria at one-thirty. There were rows and rows of kids everywhere. Everyone had on their nicest clothes.

It was crazy noisy. The metal legs of chairs scraped against the tile floors as kids shifted in their seats and whispered excitedly.

A school banner hung from the ceiling above a pull-out stage along one of the cafeteria walls. There was a podium with a microphone on the left side of the stage and a table right beside it displaying a line of trophies.

We sat down with our teachers. The teachers clutched folders full of perfect attendance and citizenship certificates for each of their classes. There was a different section roped off for our families. Clark snuck over to sit with my mom even though he was supposed to be with his class.

The principal turned on the microphone and it screeched, making its own announcement that the awards were about to begin. We quieted down. The principal cleared his throat and called the teachers up, one by one. First, they called out the awards for the pre-kindergarteners, kindergartners, first graders, second graders, third graders, fourth graders and fifth graders. Each time we were closer.

When they got to our grade they called the citizenship awards and the perfect attendance until they were all done. The principal announced the subject matter awards himself. He pulled out his folder. He called out Nora for Science, Camila for Math, and some kids from other classes for the other subjects. When he called my name, I walked up to the stage and picked up my reading award. I waited to feel the flash of my mom's camera on me and then sat back down.

The All-School Trophies were the biggest awards so he waited until the end to announce them. When our principal called out the boy's name, we weren't surprised. Roy was always the most popular boy in school. He had also brought up his grades.

Nora and I crossed our fingers, honestly wished each other luck, and let our feet dance nervously in our white sneakers.

"And this year's All-School Girl Award goes to a girl whom we're all very proud of. She's in the gifted program and in sports. Many of her fellow students admire her, and her teacher highly recommended her," the Principal paused, and I crossed my fingers so tight they turned white.

"Your All-School Girl is Ms. Chela Gonzalez. Come on up here, Chela!"

I walked up to the stage and stood next to Roy. I looked him in the eye and saw something that I couldn't name. It made me tingle even though he was just my friend. He squeezed my hand in front of the whole school and congratulated me! Everyone clapped.

It really was like standing at the top of the tallest building downtown. Except that when I looked out, my dad wasn't there. I tried not to think of it just then. Clark hugged me when I walked off the stage. I even heard him brag to his friends about his sister. We said good-bye to all our classmates and teachers. We'd already said good-bye in class, but we did it again anyway. Nora, Roy and I even made plans to see each other that summer.

Amá put her arm around my shoulder and told me she was proud of me as we walked out of the cafeteria. It was one of those times I saw her smile with all her teeth again. I smiled back. I kissed her, and told her I was proud of her too. She'd passed her driving test earlier in the week. We drove home in the pickup and skipped "Mary Service." Amá asked if we wanted to go to Whataburger, but we were stuffed from the school parties.

The first thing I saw when we got home was my dad's old bench sitting on our porch. A million feelings came over me so rapidly that they were hard to fight. It was like tripping and falling into a pit. I sat down. I knew then that my dad really wasn't coming back. He would never have missed my big day.

gusanitos

I lay in bed the next morning, thinking about how I was Apá's shadow once. When anything went wrong, Apá was my strong still oak. I ducked under his branches.

I stared at my two trophies on the dresser. I tossed and turned in bed. I didn't want to feel bad for having felt happy. I wanted to tell Apá all about my awards. I wanted to share them with him. I thought about how Apá said "Yes you can" applied to anything.

I jumped out of bed and showered. My face stared back from the bathroom mirror. I pulled on jeans and a T-shirt. The goal was to look as ordinary as possible. My fingers combed through my tangled hair as I walked to my mom's room.

A fancy-looking bottle with a delicate pump left behind by Abuelita sat on Amá's dresser. I sprayed it on. I wore it like a person wears a feeling. It wasn't that I wanted to be sad. I wore it to remember.

"Amá, I'm going now," I yelled as I pulled the door closed behind me. I'd told Amá that I was going to church to thank Diosito and that I'd come right back. She'd worry and maybe even take off her *chancla* when she realized it was only a half-truth, but it was too late. I walked out with my trophies in my backpack. I walked out with my head tucked low. I walked out with the smell of sadness.

I crossed the street into the church. I sat in one of the front pews and said a quick prayer until someone came up beside me. It was Miss Mickey. She said that she expected to see me back at "Mary Service" on Monday. I nodded, and she walked to the back of the church. I crossed myself. I walked out the side door and stood outside watching the cars drive by.

When the bus pulled up, and the bus driver pulled open the doors, I almost backed out. But his withered hands, grasping onto the steering wheel, looked like Apá's. They made me think that he was good. I pulled a carefully folded dollar from my back pocket and boarded the bus that I wasn't allowed to ride by myself.

We rode toward Everest Cemetery. It didn't seem like the kind of place where anyone would ever rest. It had fields of grass from one end to the other. It was the kind of place that made me want to kick around a soccer ball. I didn't have a soccer ball, so I sat by Apá's grave at the edge of the cemetery.

The flowers came as if by magic. The dust winds braced themselves and blew. The flowers floated grave to grave until they fell all around me. I didn't take them. I didn't wish for them to come. They just made their way. The winds blew, and I sat surrounded by flowers until the words came too.

"This is the kind of thing you don't tell anyone. You don't say it because you might just end up in that building next to the hospital with all the crazies. I won that award. You were right. It felt so good, but when I looked out at all the faces I didn't see you. I still expected to.

"The day they brought you here, I told them this wasn't where you wanted to be. You told us. You told us you wanted to be in El Florido. You told us you wanted to be in the water or in the hills. I waited for you to come home. I waited outside until even the sun fell asleep, and Silvia made me come inside. I kept thinking that what happened to you might've been a bad dream or sick joke.

"I know you would've been there if you could've. I still wanted you to know, so I came to the cemetery and put down my thirsty roots.

"Amá still cries, you know. She is hot oil in a pan, just waiting for the slightest touch to hiss and bubble. She cries without making a sound. But the other day, I saw her smile like I hadn't in a long time. She was so proud.

"Clark also cries like when he still didn't have a name. But he cries less and less. Silvia is not as mean anymore, and Angel Jr. isn't so eager to leave and forget. I know it's not right to forget, as much as it kills us.

"No, that's not rain. I'm crying. Yes. I cry too.

Don't tease me and make me laugh. I just want to lay here and listen for your heartbeat. I want to wait with you until the *gusanitos* think I am part of the soil too. I'm not disgusted by worms. You brought them home in the tequila lollipops from Juarez. Remember how we used to go to Juarez? Remember how we ate warm tortillas rolled up with salt, and you bought us pistachio ice cream?

"We were so happy. Now I'm sad when I'm sad, and sometimes I'm sad when I'm happy. I close my eyes, and you are exactly as you were. I can hear your voice.

"*'Cuando me muera no quiero que me lloren.'*

"You didn't want us to cry when you died. I don't think you meant just then. I think you knew we would cry just then. Maybe you meant you didn't want us to cry now.

"What's that you say? Yes, it's dark. I don't want to open my eyes yet. Can you see me, Apá? Are your eyes shut too? What's that you say? I am you, and you are me."

I am also me.

That's why I can't stay.

I have to get up.

I have to go home.

I got up. I walked looking at my toes. I understood that my dad wanted us to be happy. I understood because I was him, and he was me.

I looked up. The sun shone; maybe it had always been that way.

I sat on Apá's bench when I got home. I remembered the day I told him how excited I was about school. My last year in elementary school was over and so many things had happened. Some were terrible. But sixth grade didn't matter any more. I was bigger. The world was bigger. I heard the tree branches shaking their leaves loose. I heard Apá swaying in the wind, with his branches rapping loud against the windows. I smiled.

Seventh grade, eighth grade, the first day of high school, college and many more days would come. It was okay. The universe didn't feel so large and empty.